“Five p

You’ve lost five p

Quen high-fived me and I did a little mambo. I’d finally learned that move from step class, but it had taken me several classes to get it down.

Losing that weight felt good, having Quen’s hands on me felt even better. I liked him touching me. I often moved an arm or leg into his *accidentally* as I struggled with a machine during my workouts. Sometimes I struggled on purpose, and although his touching me could be considered part of his job as my personal trainer, there were times I fantasized about a different scenario....

I smiled into those chocolate eyes and tried not to lick my lips. I loved it that he called me sugar. Although weight loss and sweetener didn’t go together, we were at least making progress. I was sick and tired of being called thick, and now that his skinny ex was coming to town I needed to get the weight off. She would be my incentive.

Books by Marcia King-Gamble

Kimani Romance

Flamingo Place

Kimani Press Arabesque

Remembrance
Eden's Dream
Under Your Spell
Illusions of Love
A Reason to Love
Change of Heart
Come Fall
Come Back to Me
A Taste of Paradise
Designed for You

Kimani Press Sepia

Jade
This Way Home
Shattered Images

MARCIA KING-GAMBLE

was born on the island of St. Vincent, a heavenly place in the Caribbean where ocean and skies are the same mesmerizing blue. An ex–travel industry executive, Marcia's favorite haunts remain the Far East, Venice and New Zealand.

In her spare time, she enjoys kickboxing, step aerobics and Zumba, then winding down with a good book. A frustrated interior designer, Marcia's creativity finds an outlet in her home where nothing matches. She is passionate about animals, tearjerker movies and spicy food. She serves double duty as the director of member services at the Writers and Artists Institute in south Florida, and is the editor of *Romantically Yours*—a monthly newsletter.

To date, Marcia has written twelve novels and two novellas. She loves hearing from fans. You may contact her at Mkinggambl@aol.com, or P.O. Box 25143, Fort Lauderdale, FL 33320.

MARCIA
KING-GAMBLE

To Teresa and James Etta, owners of Nonna's Café.
Your gelato got me through and your latte kept me awake.
Thanks for leasing me free space.

ISBN-13: 978-0-373-86001-2
ISBN-10: 0-373-86001-3

ALL ABOUT ME

www.kimanipress.com

Printed in U.S.A.

Dear Reader,

I have always been fascinated by small towns. Maybe it's because I grew up on a little island where there was a sense of belonging and community that rarely exists in cities today.

Since community has always been important to me, with the help of my good friend, urban designer George Johnston (www.jtphome.com), we created Flamingo Beach. This delightful oceanfront community in Florida is a place where everyone knows everyone, and minding each other's business is a favorite pastime.

These days Flamingo Beach is in transition and fighting it every step of the way. More and more new people are moving in, condominiums are being renovated and construction is everywhere. The real estate market is booming. And Chere Adams, introduced in the first book of this series, *Flamingo Place,* is now moonlighting as a real estate agent. And as Flamingo Beach changes, so does Chere. But is a beautiful facade all that matters, or is having a solid foundation more important? I'd be interested in hearing what you think. E-mail me at Mkinggambl@aol.com or write me at P.O. Box 25143, Fort Lauderdale, FL 33320.

And be sure not to miss my next Kimani Romance title, *Down and Out in Flamingo Beach,* as Flamingo Beach, as the town's oldest citizens celebrate their centennials.

Romantically yours,

Marcia King-Gamble

Chapter 1

I knew who I was.

Chere Adams, big, beautiful, black and damn proud of it. So what was I doing at a step aerobics class at this hour when I should be in bed?

As I huffed, puffed and stared out of the big picture windows wondering when this torture would end, outside the Florida sun began to rise. In my head I pictured pork chops, scrambled eggs and grits washed down by a gallon of sweet tea. I should be wolfing down breakfast not sweating off a meal I hadn't had.

"Pick it up, ladies. Work it!"

The instructor's voice through that amplified microphone was already hurting my head. And the rap music at this hour of the morning threatened to blow an eardrum.

"One, two, three, four, five, pump those arms. Work it! Sashay to the right and pick up the pace, ladies. One…two…"

"That woman wants to seriously hurt me," I muttered to the lumbering, huffing woman next to me. "If I hear work it one more time I'm going to do something to that mic."

"Yeah, but it might well kill us to look like her," my companion in crime said between pants.

We misfits were huddled in the back of the room, bouncing up and down and pretty much falling all over ourselves.

Why I allowed myself to be talked into this class, and at such a crazy hour, was all because of Quen Abrahams, my personal trainer. I was already thinking if this was the warm-up I'd be dead by the time they started stepping. Forty-five minutes of climbing up and down steps just wasn't going to agree with Chere Adams.

I exhaled on a loud whistling breath, and tried to keep up with the dry-looking women in the front of the room making it look effortless.

Here I was, five foot six, and 225 pounds of sweating, quivering flesh trying to hold my own with women half my size. In my red sweats I looked like a raging bull, snorting and lumbering along.

"I might just have a heart attack," I wheezed. "Tell me you don't feel like your chest is on fire."

"I have a stitch in my side," my companion whined.

I had to keep reminding myself that my incentive was the eighty pounds of flesh I planned on getting rid of, and the man whose attention I wanted to get. Losing that weight would bring me down to a respectable 145 pounds. Then look out world, here comes Chere Adams.

I wanted to look just like the yellow-skinned woman in the black leotard or the brunette upfront with the fake boobs. Well not exactly like the brunette in the sports bra with her rubber hard stomach and sparkly belly button ring. She had a nonexistent butt and I liked mine, there was a helluva lot more to hold on to. But she'd gotten the attention of the muscle men in the outer room which is something I couldn't do. Actually there was only one muscle man whose attention I wanted. Quen Abrahams.

A group of awed males had their noses pressed

to the Plexiglass divider and were actually drooling. I wanted to tie a bib around their necks to stop the spit, and not the kind you got at Red Lobster, either. Food was all I could think about. What was it about the woman's nonexistent jiggle that turned them on? Must be the big boobs, it just had to be the boobs.

Mine were even bigger—40 size triple D and not full of saline either. My booty I'd been lugging around since I was twelve, and damn proudly, too. It got men's attention usually. But I had this spare tire and a couple of double chins I wanted to get rid of. That was the real reason I was here. I was sick and tired of hearing how beautiful I could be if I would only lose weight.

"It takes work, sugar!" Quentin Abrahams, my personal trainer, constantly reminded me. "Work and watching every calorie that goes into your mouth."

Easy for him to say. The man didn't know what it was like to be fat. He was built like a brick house. All muscle and sinew. And hotter than any man should be. He set me on fire.

"Okay, folks, now that our warm-up is over, time to get some real work done," the small, dark-skinned instructor chirped, bringing me back to earth. There wasn't even the slightest hitch in her breath.

"Witch!"

I wanted to kill her. Well maybe murder was a bit strong. I wanted to slap her perfect face. Here I was huffing and puffing like Farmer Jones's prize cow and there wasn't even a glimmer of moisture on "Missy Fitness's" forehead.

"What! Is she kidding?" the blonde on the other side of me groaned. "I'm done."

"Yeah, me, too," I agreed. "But looks like girlfriend wants to work us some more."

The woman I'd been speaking to earlier suddenly stopped midstep. Her breath came in great big gusts. "The treadmill's starting to look better and better." With that she left.

I looked at the wall clock. Forty three minutes of agony before the class was over.

The back of the room was slowly beginning to clear out, making big people like me with ungainly belly rolls more noticeable. The skinny minnies, dressed in pastel Lycra, sports bras and expensive jewelry were up front and center.

I should never have let Quen talk me into trying this "Step and Sculpt" class. Seven o'clock in the morning was usually when I hit the snooze button for the second or third time.

Quen said the class would be a breeze. And he

expected me to go at least three days a week. The man was doing drugs. Mind you that was over and above the sessions he and I had scheduled.

Heaving, I clutched my side. I had a stitch and wanted a drink of water badly. As I slowed down, marching in place, the class continued on, the show-offs straddling steps that had a minimum of two risers.

"This is getting old," I muttered.

The woman next to me sighed. "I hear that."

I at least had the smarts to pass on the risers. It was hard enough for me to clamber up one step much less do half hops and "V" steps. I had no clue what the instructor even meant by that. As for a sashay and mambo that was a foreign language—Spanish to me.

By some major miracle I made it through the rest of the class without collapsing. Afterward I hobbled behind several sweating women and headed for the showers.

"Looking good, Chere," Quen called after me.

The deep timbre of his voice gave me chills. It figured Quen Abrahams of all people would have to see me like this, hauling my sorry ass toward the showers. I rolled my eyes and snorted something under my breath. This had all been his idea. And I was going along with the plan because I wanted him bad.

No man deserved to look like he did at this ungodly hour. Quen was wearing a monogrammed blue short-sleeved polo shirt that stretched across his broad chest, and showed off his muscular arms to an advantage. Where the shirt V-ed there was a patch of dark hair. His khaki shorts skimmed midthigh giving me a-to-die for view of runners' legs. The same dark hairs curled over them. And his sneakers, well girlfriend, they had to be at a minimum a fourteen and they looked brand new. It was his hands that had me. They were large hands with long, nimble fingers, the nails neatly trimmed.

I wanted those hands on me. All over me. I dreamed about them.

"Must have been some workout," Quen said, preparing to move along. "You keep showing up three times a week, sugar, and we'll have you slimmed down in no time."

An hour later, my body aching, I flopped behind my desk at the *Flamingo Beach Chronicle* and began opening *Dear Jenna*'s mail. It was more of the same whining and I quickly got bored. I began daydreaming of scrambled eggs, bacon and home fries. Soon it became pork chops and chicken legs. I was that hungry.

"Hey, Chere," Jen St. George, my boss greeted as she flew in. Girlfriend was turned out as usual. She had a certain style about her that I'd tried copying but couldn't pull off. Jen's eyes were overly bright. There was a bounce to her step that made me want to strangle her. Came from sleeping with one of Flamingo Beach's hottest guys. Jen had hooked up with wisecracking radio personality, Tre Monroe. His radio audience called him D'Dawg.

"You're early," Jen said, sounding astounded. "Is something wrong?"

"Good morning to you to, missy, and no, there ain't—isn't—anything wrong."

She was right; I was always at least half an hour late. Mornings were rough on me. They made me hungry and grumpy. I was what you called a night person.

"I've been working out at the gym," I announced, twirling around. "New Years resolution, remember?" We'd both made resolutions, mine was to lose weight and exercise, Jen's was to exercise more patience. It was only the second week of January but I'd managed to keep mine. I waited for her to compliment me.

"Good for you. You're sticking to the program. Is Quen still working with you?" Jen raised a sculpted eyebrow as if she didn't think that was possible. She must think I was bluffing about losing weight?

"Yeah he is. Why?"

Jen stood and stretched. There wasn't a ripple in the midthigh skirt she wore or a bulge where her belly should be. "Nothing. I'm getting coffee. Want a cup?"

Fetching coffee was my job but I never seemed to get around to it. "Sure and while you're at it bring back a couple of them chocolate donuts the girls brought in."

Jen shook her head and wagged a finger in front of my nose. "Chocolate is totally off-limits. Those calories will go straight to our hips. I need to lose five pounds so that I can fit into my wedding gown."

I began bouncing up and down and screaming. "Jen's getting married, y'all. Tre's finally popped the question."

Several heads poked over the divider. The commotion had gotten the attention of the clerical staff who were on their desks looking over.

Jen held up her left hand for all to see. My mouth flapped open like I was catching flies. Shoot, I'd never seen a rock quite that size. D'Dawg had to be making some big bucks. I wanted one just like hers.

Oohs and aahs came from the other side of the partition. My girls had calculators for brains. They were crunching those numbers, and computing the cost of that ring right down to the last dollar.

"Congratulations!" Envy dripped from that word.

"Good luck, Jen. You caught yourself a good one."

I heard a rustle and several stifled screams.

Heads disappeared, which meant Luis Gomez, the big cheese had come in.

I was hugging Jen when Luis, stinking of cigar smoke, stuck his head in our office. "Morning, Jen," he said, totally ignoring me.

"Morning," she replied.

I stuck a tongue out behind his back. I couldn't stand him. Never could. But there wasn't a damn thing he could do about me. I had the owner of the paper, Ian Pendergrass's ear. I'd been Ian's housekeeper once; the worst one he'd ever had. But I'd served a purpose. Ian, the old goat with his randy ways deserved me.

"I'll be back with that coffee," Jen said smoothly, slipping out of my embrace.

I'd never be married. I'd never even come close. But I'd had my share of men and most of the population of Flamingo Beach thought I was a "ho." Not true. But it was good for my image for them to think that. No one should ever know that brazen-faced Chere Adams actually lacked self confidence.

And that was another reason I needed to get the

weight off. It was also the reason I'd spent two months studying like crazy for that real estate exam. I wanted to be somebody. Needed to be. I was thirty-three years old and going nowhere fast. And I wanted Quen Abrahams and babies.

I refused to think the health club manager was out of my league. Maybe he was, but a girl could try, couldn't she? I wanted the man to start thinking of me as a woman, and not just a fatso with a crazy sense of humor. We'd been friends for a long time. Now I wanted more than friendship.

Where was my coffee? I needed a pick me up and I needed one of them chocolate donuts to hold me over. Hell, I would even settle for a jelly-filled one; anything sweet. My stomach was queasy and every bone hurt.

The minutes ticked by before Jen sauntered back in minus donuts. She was carrying two mugs in her hand. She set one cup down on my desk and flipped the switch on her computer.

"Where's the food?" I demanded.

"No donuts. You're on a diet. You should be eating breakfast bars." She rummaged through her drawer and flipped a couple at me.

I caught them, glared at her and bit right through the wrapper. I was that hungry. Easy for her to say

"You're on a diet." She was built like an athlete with curves in all the right places. That glowing coffee complexion came from nights of good loving. Tre Monroe was delivering and I was getting zilch. Nada.

"How are your real estate classes coming?" Jen asked, after she was settled in and staring at her monitor.

It would be pointless to lie. In a town the size of Flamingo Beach everyone knew everyone's business and what they didn't know they made up.

"I passed the real estate and property management exam," I said, proudly sticking out my triple Ds. "Now I am officially a full-fledged Realtor."

"Good for you. Will you be juggling two jobs then, or will you be quitting on me?"

Better to play it cool and keep my mouth shut. Jen didn't have to know I had high aspirations; one of them being to get the credit I deserved at the *Chronicle*. I didn't want her job, I just wanted equal billing. *Dear Jenna and Chere,* sounded sweet to me.

"You know I can't afford to quit," I said smiling brightly. She was after all still my boss. "I need a regular salary. Besides who said I didn't like my job."

One side of Jen's lips curled up. "I thought you were bored opening mailing and cataloguing it."

"Who said I was bored?"

She cut her eyes at me. I didn't have her fooled.

I wasn't exactly bored, but I did have a short attention span. I hated sitting for hours. Plus much of the advice Jen dished out came from me. I knew everything there was to know in Flamingo Beach. And even if the people who wrote in didn't sign their real names, it was easy to figure. Nothing but nothing escaped me.

I dug into a drawer and found a letter opener, no point ruining my nails. Manicures were expensive. Especially those that had fancy artwork and sequins on them. This week mine had dolphins jumping. I'd turned into a Florida girl through and through.

"You set a date for the wedding?" I asked, my stomach rumbling thinking of that wedding cake with strawberries, fresh cream and icing.

"Tre and I will do that this weekend."

It sounded to me like Tre Monroe was delaying committing. Not that I would tell Jen that. He'd been the beach's most eligible bachelor up until missy here, from Ashton snatched him up. They'd hated each other on sight. Then somewhere along the way that hatred had turned to love. Now the buzz was they were living together.

"What's going to happen to your apartment?" I asked, partially because I was curious, and partially because I needed to find out if she wanted to rent. Heck I was a Realtor plus I had my own ulterior motive.

"I'm thinking about renting."

I wound a lock of weaved auburn hair around a jeweled fingernail and thought about how to play this. I needed a place to live. My landlady claimed her daughter and her kid were moving back to Flamingo Beach. She'd given me notice to start looking.

If I put my stuff in storage, and moved into Jen's fancy apartment, it might work. Flamingo Place was the type of upscale complex that could do wonders for my new image. And Jen's waterfront digs were to die for. I just couldn't afford to pay what she was paying.

"When are you thinking of leasing?" I asked.

She crossed one skinny leg over the other. Jen had that polished look I was striving for but couldn't quite pull off. If you weighed two hundred and twenty-five pounds and squeezed into a midthigh skirt and three-inch stilettos, you looked like a hooker. You got lots of attention but for all the wrong reasons.

"Do you know someone who might be interested?" Jen asked, "I could make the apartment available immediately. I'm spending more and more time at Tre's place and an empty apartment isn't a good thing."

She'd confirmed they were more or less living together. Opportunity only knocked once. I took a deep breath and stepped through the door.

"I might be interested."

"You?"

Jen sounded like she didn't think I was serious.

I explained what had happened with my landlady.

"Hmm," she said, stroking her chin. "But what would you do with all of your stuff?"

"Put it in storage. It would only be for a couple of months. I don't even know if I can afford the rent." I played my ace card. "There is a plus to having me live there."

"And what is that?"

"Being that I'm officially in the real estate business, and I know a lot of people, I could keep an eye out for a tenant. You'd be my very first client."

"Hmm."

All these "hmms" were beginning to annoy me. I might be a lowly peon at the *Chronicle* but I was well connected. Jen knew exactly who'd gotten me this job; Ian Pendergrass himself. She also knew I'd introduced her to a lot of important people.

"Could you manage to pay say six hundred

dollars a month?" Jen asked. "That would be half of my mortgage. I'll pick up the other half until you find me a tenant."

"I could pay five," I countered, crossing my fingers behind my back. Five hundred would be a steal for Jen's two-bedroom water-view apartment, and I would be able to put aside a few hundred per month. She didn't have to know the rattrap I lived in was costing me close to a thousand.

I'd slaved to make the place pretty. The toilets leaked and the pictures on the walls hid holes and flaking plaster. Even the partitions were thin. During the late hours you could hear the neighbors' bedsprings squeak. I'm sparing you the graphics. You don't want to know.

"Okay, we'll agree on five."

I squealed loudly and moved in to hug her.

The phone rang and we both reached for it.

"This is *Dear Jenna,*" Jen said in her professional voice. I was surprised when she handed the receiver to me.

"New boyfriend? He's got a sexy voice."

I wish.

"Hello, this is Chere," I said, the elocution classes I attended one night a week finally kicking in. Plus

I remembered the reprimand I'd received from Jen for saying, "Hey."

"Just a reminder, tomorrow morning at seven. Don't mess up." It was Quen Abrahams again. I'd missed one session two weeks ago and trust me I'd heard about it. I'd needed my beauty sleep and I'd overslept.

I groaned. I'd forgotten all about making that appointment. Plus I didn't have the extra sixty dollars to pay him even though he was giving me a break.

Quen was not only Flamingo Place's health club manager and on-site nutritionist, but was doing me a favor personally training me.

"My legs are killing me. Every bone hurts," I whined.

"It'll get better," Quen said in that voice that reminded me of nights when the temperature in Florida dipped into the fifties and you broke out the wine and Barry White. "Did you weigh in today?"

I grunted something. I'd totally forgotten.

I could feel Jen's eyes on me and sensed the wheels turning. Everyone thought I was easy and had a string of men. They should only know what it took for me to sleep with a man. Courage. Ian and I hadn't exactly slept together. The old geezer liked to look and touch.

"I'll see you tomorrow at the club then. Seven o'clock sharp, remember," Quen said.

"I'll be there." I blew a kiss through the mouthpiece. "Love you, too."

Under my breath I muttered, "slave driver," and slammed down the phone.

Chapter 2

Crabby because I was still hungry, I clomped home and had a salad for dinner. I was starving. I stuck my head in the refrigerator, found a turkey leg in one of those Ziploc bags and yanked it out.

I zapped that leg in the microwave and quickly wolfed it down. Food never tasted so good. Afterward I sat down and made a list of what I needed to do to improve myself.

The phone rang just as I was thinking how much all this reinventing was going to cost.

"Talk to me," I said, picking up the receiver.

"Chere?" Sheena, one of my girls greeted in her usual high-pitched squeak. She didn't wait for me to acknowledge her but began babbling away. Meanwhile my stomach was still rumbling. I considered having another piece of turkey just to quiet things down.

"So did I hear right?" Sheena yakked. "Your boss is taking a stroll down the aisle with our favorite disk jockey?" That girl didn't miss a thing.

"You heard right."

"When's the wedding?"

"I don't know." I didn't want to talk about any wedding unless it was mine.

My short answers didn't bother Sheena one bit. She was off and running. "What's happening with your real estate? You selling any houses yet?"

"I just passed the test a week ago. Cut me some slack," I said irritably. I wasn't going to say one word about my two clients. That news would be all over town in a Flamingo Beach minute and I didn't want to be jinxed.

"Then you must not have sold anything," she said. Sheena could be a bitch at times. "I hear they're looking for part time help selling or renting properties at Flamingo Place. Manny Varela is the property manager. You want me to put in a good word for you?"

"No, thanks. I know Manny. I can speak for myself."

Sheena had been sleeping off and on with Manny for over a year. Sleeping with men that weren't hers was Sheena's favorite pastime. It was an ego thing. True, Manny with his jet-black hair, olive complexion and expensive designer suits wasn't bad. But it was the Benz he drove that made him a catch.

"Well let me know if you change your mind," Sheena said, "And call me the minute you hear something." She hung up.

These next few months were going to be devoted to me. I planned on losing weight, getting my man and starting a new career, and not necessarily in that order. Earlier, I'd placed a big toe on the bathroom scale and was pleasantly surprised to see the number was lower. Growing braver, I'd given the scale my whole weight. I still had eighty-three pounds to go, but losing two pounds for me was a big deal and should be celebrated.

Over the years I'd pretty much convinced myself that being big worked for me. I hadn't lacked admirers. What you don't know is there's a slew of "chubby chasers" out there; men who think being full figured is hot. They weren't necessarily what I was looking for but what I got. My expectations were set way high. This year I'd made resolutions; one being to get Quen Abrahams.

Quen with the corded arms and strong thigh muscles also came with a degree and ambition, and he could string two sentences together while flashing you a gut-wrenching smile. Since I had a degree and had worked damn hard to get it, I needed a man who was my equal, especially if he was going to father my child.

Tomorrow we were working out of Jen's condo; a good thing, too, because I'd probably be dead after my session with Quen. During lunch I had an interview with Manny Varela, the property manager Sheena mentioned earlier. Like she said, his sales and leasing office was looking for part-timers. I needed a second job and I needed it quickly. These personal training sessions were pricey and diet food cost money.

Now I had just fifteen minutes to get to my elocution class. The class had been advertised in one of those inserts you get in the Sunday paper. It was a continuing education course given by one of the neighboring high schools and aimed at a certain type of person. Although it cost $150, I whipped out my credit card and paid. I was investing in myself. I couldn't think of anyone better.

Deep down I'd always known if I wanted to be somebody I'd need to walk the walk and talk the talk.

Not that I was turning my back on my roots, mind you. Like I said I knew who I was and I didn't need to prove anything to anybody.

I made the ten-minute drive in five. And yes, I admit I have a lead foot. Class had just started when I tromped in and with a "hey" to the homies sitting next to me, I plopped onto a seat at the back of the room.

"You didn't miss much," the woman who'd told me she was an administrative assistant, but thought she was a CEO whispered to me.

"Good."

The instructor, a proper-looking man who still wore a bow tie, and who had to be gay, was in the middle of taking attendance. He gave us a stern look. Since Adams was at the beginning of the alphabet he'd already passed over me.

I had nothing else to do so I looked around the room to see if there were any dropouts. Yup. This was the third session and the group was a lot smaller than I remembered. The class was supposedly aimed at foreigners and business types; people needing to learn to speak right.

The first two sessions had been jam-packed; now the only people I recognized were the married couple and the immigrants from Cuba, who barely spoke English, and in my opinion required more than "elocution." Then there was the freckled guy from New "Joisey" who wanted to be friends. I called him, "Dese, Dems and Dose," but not to his face of course. I wasn't that stupid. Not that I was in a position to make fun of anybody.

The two homeboys who'd greeted me were still hanging in. They looked out of place in their oversize jeans riding low on the hips, with their undershorts sticking out over the top. In this case something big was at stake here, like money.

I grew up with the language of the street, which meant you said what you thought and punctuated with some well chosen cuss words to get your point across loud and clear. Jen, my boss had been forever after me to clean up my act. And I was trying. Talking like you had marbles in your mouth worked for her so why not me? It had landed her a cushy job. I'd decided if I was going to be selling real estate to all kinds of people no one needed to know I was black, at least not right off.

"Ms. Adams," the instructor called, pulling me back to reality. I didn't know the man even knew my name.

"Wassup, Mr. Cummings?"

He peered at me over ridiculous half-moon glasses and sniffed.

"Yes, Mr. Cummings?" he corrected.

"Yes, Mr. Cummings," I obediently repeated.

A finger beckoned me to join him up front. As I plodded toward him, he turned to write on the blackboard. I was starting to feel like I was back in fourth grade when "the fat girl" was being singled out.

"Please translate these phrases in the queen's English for the rest of the class," Cummings said, handing me his chalk.

"Say what?"

Shoot, queen's English? The United States did not have a queen, at least not the last time I looked. I scrunched up my nose and stared at the strange little man. The homeboys cracked up. People were howling and holding their sides.

Cummings sniffed loudly and wagged a finger. "This is exactly what I mean. Those types of expressions have no place in everyday language. You are here to learn to speak English, and that includes the use of proper grammar. You are here to articulate."

"Yo, man. You trying to teach us to conversate," one of the homeboy's in the back shouted.

That produced another round of laughter.

Mr. Cummings gave him his stern look.

"You must eliminate all urban slang from your vocabulary, Ms. Adams. Now please continue."

Yup. I was being made an example of. Lucky for me, I was wearing one of my hot little J Lo outfits, well maybe not so little. It was size 3X. I was working it. Rather than writing, I repeated out loud what I thought Cummings wanted to hear. He corrected me in his snotty manner and I slunk back to my chair.

The remainder of the two-hour class passed quickly. The homeboys had their turn, as did the Cuban couple. Cummings was mean. I'd almost decided I wasn't being singled out. I knew people judged you by both your appearance and the way you spoke. They assumed if you were a big girl you were a slow, stupid ox. But being big had always been advantageous for me. My sense of humor and big mouth had made me popular in school and gotten me through.

The way I saw it, Cummings's class was keeping me off the street these days. Before that I'd spent one night a week at the Haul Out. Not because I was a big drinker, but because it was a sure way of catching up on who was doing who. All that time hanging out got me a big fat nothing except the occasional pick-up, then when he found out I was on lockdown I promptly got dumped. This elocution class would at least help me build a future.

I left thinking that even though Mr. Cummings had a stick up his ass, he might be onto something.

I'd only been home about fifteen minutes, and was thinking about going to bed when my telephone rang.

"Yeah?"

"Hey, sweet thang."

Who the hell was this?

"Do I know you?"

The man chuckled. "Baby, how could you forget the best lover you've ever had? This is Richard."

"Richard who?"

Why was he acting like I knew him, like we were close?

A long pause followed as he tried to pick up his ego from the floor. "Richard Dyson, baby, the owner of Dyson Luxury Limousines."

Oh, that Dick! Rich Richard. Obnoxious Richard. Richie Rich who thought his Platinum American Express card bought him any woman. The last time he'd phoned was months ago. It had been late at night, he'd been drunk and on a booty-call spree. "What do you want Dickie?"

"Can't a man touch base with a beautiful woman just to see how she's doing?"

"It's been three months since you and I spoke."

"Doesn't mean I'm not thinking about you, sweetness. What are you doing now? I'd like to come over."

"Going to bed," I answered. "Without you. Good night, Dick."

"Wait! Wait! How about dinner tomorrow night? You pick the place."

"I'll get back to you."

I hung up while he was still talking.

I used Dyson's Luxury Limousines when I was out to make an impression or didn't want to drive. Like the time I attended my cousin's wedding and knew that the sight of her in a white wedding dress, complete with trailing veil, would make me drink. Richard owed me because if it hadn't been for my contacts, he'd never have gotten the *Flamingo Beach Chronicle*'s account. Then Jen got Richard the WARP account through Tre, her fiancé, who now used Dyson's exclusively to pick up the people he hosted.

Richard and I had gone out a time or two when I was lonely, and being with him seemed better than being alone. He'd dropped big money on those dinners. Now I'm starting to sound like I'm a gold digger. Fast-talking Dickie isn't too bad to look at and he liked his women big. Since the way to my heart is definitely through my stomach I thought I'd give him a shot. Feed me and I'll listen to you bray on any topic. Richard's gold card had taken a beating on those meals.

I yawned. My bed waited. I had to be up at the crack of dawn and I needed my beauty sleep. I was already planning tomorrow's outfit in my head. As my grandmother used to say, "fat does not have to mean sloppy." She was one smart old lady.

After I'd left class, I stopped at a discount store and splurged on a new workout outfit. The peanuts I got paid didn't get me into Macy's. I hadn't gone hog wild with the colors and although it killed me, I passed on zebra stripes and polka dots, sticking to black. Black was slimming. I bought two pairs of capris and an oversized T-shirt and spiced up the outfit with hot pink socks and a matching cap that said, Love Handles All.

I was doing this for Quen Abrahams. I'd noticed the types of women he went for. They were fit, trim and looked like they stepped off magazine covers. I was going to be one of those women soon.

Bedtime. I was getting overtired and punchy.

A god-awful racket woke me next morning. It sounded like a freight train was roaring through my head. I hit the snooze button, sat up and looked at the clock. I had exactly one half hour to crawl into my outfit, plug in the curling iron and throw in some curls.

By the time I left my apartment I had ten minutes to get across town. It wasn't even summer yet but it was hotter than hell in Florida, this promised to be a steamer of a day. The air-conditioning in my car was on the blink and I would be feeling it. Trying not to think about that, I wedged myself behind the wheel of my Honda, cranked up the engine, and lowered the window. I roared into that parking lot with a full minute to spare.

Quen was waiting in one of the workout rooms. He had on black track pants with a stripe on the side, and a body hugging T-shirt with a hot pink flamingo emblem that matched my socks.

"Morning," he said, glancing at his watch. "You're right on time. Cute getup."

"Thanks." Boyfriend sure as hell made my mouth go dry. It was going to be one painful hour and not just because of the exercise session.

Quen was one of those delicious, dark brown men, with a smooth complexion and square jaw. Everything about him squeaked cleanliness. He had wide shoulders, a tapered waist and hands just as scrupulously clean as the rest of him.

I set my fanny pack in the corner and made my way to the machine in the corner that he pointed out. The contraption made me think of that guillotine I'd read about in my English class, Madame Defart or something. Grimacing, I managed to mount the thing while he barked orders.

"Tuck your stomach in and sit up straight. Your legs go under not over."

Quen stood beside me, his hands on my flesh, showing me where everything went. My stomach fluttered and the parts below pulsed. I closed my eyes and inhaled citrus. God I loved how he smelled. Gotta get me a piece of him. Soon.

Concentrate, Chere. Forget about the fact that you want to eat this man whole.

I concentrated letting the pain of muscles I hadn't used in years numb my brain. There was definitely more than sixty minutes in an hour when your whole body ached. Finally it was over. I was crippled but done. Now I needed a wheelchair to get back to my car.

"Good workout," Quen said as we cooled down. Of course he could say that he hadn't been the one peddling or rowing. He hadn't even broken a sweat. "Come with me to my office."

I would go with him anywhere. I limped down a

hallway to a glass-enclosed box that was as neat as he looked. A Formica desk held a tray with only a few pieces of paper stacked on top. A filing cabinet was angled in one corner. Framed photos of fitness gurus adorned the walls, and in another corner was one of those medical scales. Tell me he wasn't planning to have me get on some scale. I liked the guy, okay, wanted him badly, but he didn't need to see how much I weighed.

I took a whiff at my pits. Phew! My deodorant was a thing of the past.

Quen waved me into the chair across from his desk. He crossed over to the filing cabinet removed a card and handed it to me. His finger brushed mine.

Zap. Zap. Zap. His touch was electric and I was lit.

"What you got here?" I asked, turning the card over.

"A list of suggested foods to stay away from. I'm a nutritionist, remember? Normally I give these cards to my clients after weighing them in."

We were back to weight again. I had no intention of putting one toe on that scale, not with him standing there. Besides, I'd only hired him to do the personal training bit. I didn't need no menu.

"Thanks," I said, the card still in my hand. I

smiled at him. "You can hook me up with some menus soon as I can afford it. If my real estate career takes off then you and I are in business."

Quen sat behind his desk, legs propped on the surface, ankles crossed. His brown eyes twinkled. He must find me amusing.

"Consider that a gift," he said. "So when did you become a real estate agent? Last I knew you were working for the *Chronicle.*"

"I still am."

"Hmm."

I looked him square in the eye. God, just gazing at him made me want to eat him alive. "That job barely pays the bills so I had to do something. I got my first client yesterday."

"Congratulations. Want another?"

I perked up immediately. Was he teasing me or what? "I'm open."

"Available?"

I swear he was flirting and dang I wanted him to.

I needed another client. Heck I needed several more clients to make this work.

Quen took his legs off the desk and rolled his chair forward, looking at me intently. "I own three apartments in the Flamingo Place complex," he confided. "I need two renters."

"You don't say?"

This was news to me. I knew Quen was smart I just didn't know he had business sense. Boyfriend was a real entrepreneur.

"I bought them at the insiders' price when the buildings were transitioning from rentals to condos."

Forgetting about sweat and my fear of B.O., I leaned in closer.

"Betcha I could move those condos for you. Are you looking to sell or to rent?"

"Rent right now. I figured if I can hold on to them for a couple of years I could make a small fortune."

"And they're all waterfront?" My mind was calculating both possibilities and commissions.

"Yes. I'm keeping the corner unit for myself. It's the biggest with the best view."

Excitement surged through me. When I moved into Jen's place we would be neighbors. And if I were his real estate agent we would be talking regularly. I won't need an excuse to call him. I'd be more than the fat woman he was helping to lose weight.

Quen and I would be agent and client, and later boyfriend and girlfriend. Fantasy was already taking over.

I was going to be late for work. I stood.

"You're my friend," I said. "For friends I work

miracles. You let me rent those apartments and I'll cut my commission in half."

"Three months," Quen countered. "You've got three months to find me suitable tenants." He named a figure he hoped to get for rent. I blinked. I needed to make it happen.

He was shrewd. I admired that in a man.

I pumped his hand when what I really wanted to do was the raise the roof dance. You know, palms in the air, booty swinging. I'd acquired my second client and in only two days.

Cha-Ching!

Chapter 3

"Why should Flamingo Place Realty hire you?" Manny Varela asked me as if we were strangers.

He sat in this big swivel chair behind a huge glass desk, making notes on a pad with an expensive-looking pen.

I almost didn't answer. I had nothing to prove to Manny. We'd been friends ever since nursery school. Manny and I had spent endless times playing "show and tell." Truth is Manny has little to show, but he does like to tell. I know every inch of his olive body and he knows every layer of mine.

In the thirty-plus years we'd known each other, we'd done everything short of sleeping together. And believe me when I tell you his weenie is teenie. Sheena told me it still hasn't grown up.

Okay, okay. I was supposed to take him seriously. This was an interview, if I got the job Manny would be my boss. He'd left Flamingo Beach after high school and gone away to college. He'd returned years later claiming to have experience in real estate and property management, and he'd worked his way up from agent to big shot.

"You know anyone who knows this town better than me?" I answered, batting my lashes at Manny.

His big white capped teeth flashed an acknowledgment. They were a new addition that must have cost him a fortune.

"Having you work for Flamingo Place Realty would certainly be a plus. You know everyone there is to know in town. And their business," he added.

Smooth. Yeah Manny was as smooth as the slicked back black hair on his head. He tapped the black and gold pen he was holding against the desk's glass surface.

"Aren't you still working at the *Chronicle?*" he asked, stroking his chin. "How are you going to swing two jobs?"

I shot him my mean look, which meant narrowing my eyes and sticking out my bottom lip. "Didn't you say this was part-time?"

"Yes, weekends and such. You did well on the real estate test, plus you're a talker. That's to be taken into consideration."

Enough of this cat and mouse B.S. "Do I get the job or what?"

"I'm thinking."

I'd brought Manny a copy of my notification that I'd passed the test, just in case he didn't believe me. Either he wanted to hire me or he didn't not. So what was there to think about?

"You still dating Lizzie Smith?" I asked, playing my ace card.

By the way he jumped out of that chair you would have thought a gnat had stung him.

"Off and on. Why?"

I pushed back a handful of store bought hair off my face, and did a chicken neck. "Ain't you and Lizzie exclusive. So how come you doing Sheena?"

Manny needed to know I knew about Sheena. Let him read between the lines and not underestimate me. If he didn't hire me I'd be chatting with Lizzie.

"I could give you a try..."

Manny wasn't stupid.

I bounced up and down and began screaming. I threw my arms around his neck and pressed his muscular body against mine. "You the man, Manny. You won't be disappointed."

He gave me a little push away from him on account of the weenie becoming less teenie.

"There is a but." He gulped.

"Yeah?" He was beginning to sweat. That white starched shirt had rings around the armpits.

"Uh…things are fairly casual here in Florida, but if you're selling real estate you can't look too wild. A personal shopper might help you get more pulled together."

Suck it in, girl. You got the job. That's what counts.

I loved my look. I might be out there sometimes but it was me. I liked being wild. And I didn't need to lay out money for some 3X pants outfit or one of them stuffy suits. But if Manny wanted me to get a personal shopper then I'd consult Jen. She'd been threatening forever to give me a makeover. And it wouldn't cost me a thing.

"Well what do you say?" Manny asked, glancing at his buffed nails and then back at me.

"What do I say about what?"

"About starting this weekend?"

I gave him another hug almost knocking him over. "You're the man."

"It's strictly commission," Manny warned. "You'll have an office and a desk in that cubicle. And you'll need to be on time. Understand?"

"Do I get a secretary who's goin' to screen my calls?"

"You're pushing it, Cherrie." He called me Cherrie to annoy me. "I'm just trying you out for size."

Back to the weight thing or was it just my imagination.

I curled up one side of my lip, kinda like a dog does and snarled, "Okay, Saturday it is, first thing. Thank you, Manny." Then I wiggled my fingers and sailed off.

I had to pinch myself. I was now a full-fledged real estate agent and already I had properties to show: Quen's two apartments. Next on the agenda, business cards.

A big fat smile creased my face as I crossed the parking lot. Things sure were looking up. I'd lost two pounds this week, gotten two clients and had a new job. Now I needed to focus on getting that promotion at the *Flamingo Beach Chronicle*.

It might require Ian Pendergrass. Jen wasn't about

to hand over her column to me, and truthfully I didn't want it; at least not all of it. I just wanted to get credit where credit was due. Talking to the editor, Luis Gomez, would be useless. Luis was too much of a wuss to do anything about it.

I sat planning my strategy while eating lunch. Yuck, I hated canned tuna fish and what could a measly boiled egg do to satisfy real hunger? I found a guest spot in Jen's condo lot and swung the Honda into it. There were days Jen liked us to work from her condo and today just happened to be one of those days.

"So how did it go?" Jen asked, the moment she let me into her apartment.

"I got the job."

"Good for you. By the way that stack's getting huge," she said, pointing to the growing pile of letters in her box. Letters I hadn't the time or desire to read, though it was supposedly my job to tell her which ones required her attention.

She was already banging away on that laptop of hers.

I'd made no secret about this job interview. I'd been crying poverty for a long time. I'd threatened to find a job as an exotic dancer; sliding up and down poles and wagging your tits in some horny guy's face paid bucks.

I'd told Jen I'd give the required notice if something good came along. I didn't want her thinking I would always be here; the loyal assistant that she'd promised to take on a cruise and then dumped. Maybe if she thought I was going to walk I could finagle a big fat raise. Nobody else in town could provide the kind of inside information I could.

Grabbing the pile of letters, I made myself comfortable on the couch. A bag of potato chips would have been perfect right now. But for now I would have to settle for an awesome view of the open bay and fantasize what it would be like to live on some fancy boat with a deck hand slobbering all over me. Mentally, I had already moved in.

"Chere! Letters!"

"Okay, okay," I jumped up and made a half-hearted attempt to read. I waved a letter at her. "This one's from Camille Lewis complaining about Winston."

Camille was Jen's neighbor from hell. She and her husband lived in 5D. Camille was a nosy, loud West Indian woman who loved getting into peoples' business. Winston, the quiet, long-suffering husband, had pretty much thrown in the towel. Why Winston put up with Camille no one knew. Some speculated she did cartwheels in bed.

"Read it to me," Jen ordered, a pencil clenched between her teeth.

My painted on eyebrows arched, and with some satisfaction, I read aloud. I hated Camille and she hated me.

"Dear Jenna,

I have lost respect for my husband. He's a puppy dog and just follows me around. The worse I behave, the more loyal he is. I push to get a reaction, any reaction. He's no longer interested in sex. All he wants to do is sleep. He's a man of a certain age. Do you think he needs Viagra? I don't want to leave him. Should I get a lover?"

Jen frowned. "Why do you think it's Camille?"

"'Cause there ain't nobody in this town she can talk to about her situation. Nobody trusts her."

"There isn't anyone in this town she can talk to," Jen corrected.

"Whatever."

I was trying to clean up my act, really I was. It's just when you've talked a certain way for so long, it's comfortable for you.

"Give me that." Jen reached out a hand.

I handed her the letter and went back to reading the others. I was bored, and sick to death of reading about other people's problems. But something made me look up. I froze. On top of Jen's desk was a pile of bridal magazines.

It was a sad reminder that I wasn't getting any younger. My biological clock was going tick-tock, and I had no man around. Time to hit the john before I got weepy.

"Where are you going?" Jen called after me as I wobbled down the hallway in my three-inch platforms. "Stay away from the refrigerator."

She knew me that well. And yeah, I was beginning to feel faint. The lousy boiled egg and tuna minus mayonnaise had made me hungrier. I blinked a couple of times and dry-eyed, doubled back.

"I'm taking the tour of my new home," I said, trying to sound jolly. Fat girls are supposed to always be happy. I wasn't. "When can I move in?"

"When do you want to move in?"

"Tomorrow." I was half kidding. But this was living in the lap of luxury compared to how I lived. My landlady wanted me out. I had a running toilet and a broken dishwasher that hadn't been fixed in weeks and I'd been slow on my rent.

"How about week after next? That'll make it close

to the end of the month," Jen said. "It'll give me time to move some things into Tre's place, the rest of the stuff I'll put in storage."

"Yeah, two weeks will work. I need a favor."

"I'm not lending you money."

I cut my eyes at her. I'd only borrowed money from her once and I'd offered to pay it back with interest when my numbers came in. She'd refused to accept anything more than the loan.

"Take me shopping."

"Sure. Do you have a credit card you can still use?"

I shot her a dirty look. "I need business clothes. Manny says if I'm to work in real estate I need to dress the part."

"Manny is right. We could go shopping after you finish reading those letters. I'll even treat you to dinner at the Pink Flamingo later."

"Okay you got it."

I had my teeth set for plump pork chops, garlic smashed potatoes and at least three buttered rolls.

"What are you going to do about your hair?" Jen asked, circling me.

"What's wrong with my hair?"

"Big hair's dated, hides your pretty face."

I was sick to death of hearing about my pretty face. I'd been hearing about it all my life, that and my weight. Enough already, it was enough to make a body do some serious eating.

Getting rid of my weave meant I'd need a relaxer and a cut. Jen knew how much I made. Couldn't she let the weave slide? I'd have to take out a second mortgage just to improve my appearance and I didn't own a home.

"All right, all right. But I don't want to look like those old ladies with the helmet hair and tight curls."

"What about going natural. Just add a little texturizer to your hair and you should be fine. If you play up your eyes and highlight your cheekbones, I say move over Halle, Chere's the new girl in town." She laughed and I laughed with her.

"Okay back to work."

Jen plopped down in her chair, her attention again on her monitor. Her fingers flew across the keyboard. "What have I got for the Sunday column?"

I snorted. At least she could say "we," and acknowledge my contribution.

Four hours later, my car was filled with shopping bags from the three stores that Jen insisted we go into. I'd been talked into buying black everything and I wasn't feeling the clothes, reminded me of a funeral director. I'd turned into a Florida girl and I liked my vibrant colors. But I put on a happy face and pretended to go ga-ga over the slacks, skirt and jacket she'd picked out, all in the same boring black.

Jen even made me buy old lady pumps. You know the kind with three inch heels and round tip that ladies with varicose veins wore. "Orthopedic" shoes I called them.

By the time we were through shopping I was way over my credit card limit. I had to talk the bank into upping the amount. Now I was in serious hock. I'd better sell some houses quick.

"I'm starving," Jen announced as we pulled into a vacant spot in back of the Pink Flamingo.

I hadn't eaten anything since lunch so I was more than starving. Even the fluttering fake flamingos on the restaurant's ceiling looked like they might make good barbeque.

On a Wednesday night, the place was jumping. The hostess, a hot Latino woman who thought she was better than everyone, flirted with the restaurant manager, Rico. She managed to peel herself off of him to greet us.

"We want a table in the bar area," Jen said not consulting me. Guess I wasn't good enough to be taken into the restaurant.

Whipping long jet-black hair off her face, the hostess asked, "Is it just the two of you?"

"You see anybody else?"

Jen shushed me loudly before I could say something real smart-assed.

"Follow me."

I clomped along behind them, looking around to see who was there. Drinks must be half-priced because the bar was jumping. Spotting Chet Rabinowitz, the mayor's son, I waved. He and his lover, Harley, gave me the hand sign that meant "call us," soon.

My girls were out in full force, the ones I ran into at the curl and weave; those who were forever running their mouths. Most were on their way to being hooked up or laid.

We slid into a booth. Jen and I faced each other. I was all talked out and just wanted the menu. I stabbed my finger at the first thing I saw. Jen barely glanced at hers before tossing it aside.

"I know what I'm having," she announced. "A Cobb salad."

"Cobb what?"

"Salad. Nice, healthy and will justify my glass of wine."

"I'm having ribs with barbecued sauce."

She slapped my hand. "No you're not."

"Am too."

"Don't let me slap you. Didn't you say something about having lost two pounds?"

I stuck out my tongue. "Fine, fried chicken with collard greens on the side."

"We'll have two Cobb salads," Jen said when the waitress came over. Wine for me and water for her."

Who died and left her boss. That's right, she was my boss.

"Isn't that Quen seated at the bar?" Jen mumbled out of the side of her mouth.

"Where?"

My palms became sweaty and my stomach began to rumble. All on account of hunger of course. The walls around me wavered, changing from Flamingo pink to floral.

"Think the woman seated next to him is a date?"

Now why did she have to say that? Quen on a date was bound to upset me. I'd want to poison the witch.

I kept my face blank, tossed a glance in the direction of the bar, and damn near flew out of my seat.

Sheena, the "ho," was sitting next to my man.

Not for long. I was on my way over.

Chapter 4

"Hi, Quen, Sheena," I said, sidling up next to them.

"Hey, sugar," Quen's megawatt smile washed over me and I melted. "Where did you come from?"

Sheena's glare clearly told me I wasn't wanted and that made me madder. I pointed over to Jen who was eyeing the scene over the top of her wineglass and making sure to keep her distance. She knew I was volatile.

"Ladies night, eh?" Quen said his eyes twinkling. "What are you drinking?"

"Water because of you." I wasn't sure if it was an

offer to buy or whether Quen was testing me. I stood my ground and gave my friend the evil eye. "You two got something going?"

"Do we have something going?" Quen put the question right back to Sheena.

"We could."

So that's the way it was. They were working their way toward hooking up. Over my dead body!

I planted myself firmly between them. "Quen and I have a breakfast date, don't we, Quen?

"You know it, sugar. Try not to cheat, at least not a lot." He winked at me.

Sheena's gaze dripped poison. Since neither one of them asked me to sit down and Quen didn't follow through on the drink offer, there was nothing left for me to do than crawl back to where I came from. But I'd put Sheena on notice, and that was what I'd set out to do.

The salads had arrived: a few measly pieces of lettuce, chopped egg yolk, whites and luncheon meat cut in bite-size cubes—at least that's what it looked like. Pitiful.

"So what did you find out?" Jen asked carefully.

"That they're not dating. Sheena's out to get laid."

"And that comes as a big surprise." Jen's hazel

eyes inspected me carefully over the rim of that wine glass. "Think Quen will bite?"

I snorted. "I don't know and I don't care."

"Sure you do. Look I wasn't going to tell you this but I heard Quen's ex-wife might be moving back to Flamingo Beach?"

"What!" I was the one who heard all of the news first. So how come Jen had one up on me?

"Tre was in Joya's Quilts the other day picking up a gift for his mother. Granny J waited on him. She told him her granddaughter, her namesake, was coming to town for a visit."

Joya back in Flamingo Beach meant only one thing. Trouble. It had taken Quen at least a year to get over her.

I didn't like the idea that size-two Joya with her great big gray eyes and delicate ways was going to be my competition. She'd dumped Quen, then gotten hired by an airline, and moved to L.A. where we all hoped she'd stay. I wondered if Quen knew Joya was coming back to town. I'd fish around and see what I could find out tomorrow.

"So what do you think?" I asked the tall blonde in the capris and halter top that her boobs were falling out of. She'd been mincing around the five-room apartment for over an hour, poking her head into every nook and cranny. I was still trying to figure out what she was looking for. I mean the condo was unfurnished.

Grandpa accompanying her, I had pegged as a sugar daddy. He was real old and Daisy kept rubbing those big nipples against his arm and whining, "Charlie, I just don't know. I'm thinking we should hold out for the penthouse. You'd be much more comfortable."

"I don't have any penthouses available," I said, trying not to sound disgusted, which I was. "The buildings in Flamingo Place have seven floors. You can put your name on the waiting list for a villa if you want but they're under construction. If you're looking for waterfront the starting price is in the high seven hundreds."

Up until now I was doing really well; maintaining my professionalism and elocuting all over the place. Manny Varela and Mr. Cummings would be proud of me. What I really wanted to do was slap the bitch so hard her collagen lips wobbled.

Daisy didn't blink an eye. "Villa? Did you say villa? And it's waterfront."

Charlie's adams apple bobbed. "Honey, it's not like we plan on being here in the summer. This two-bedroom condominium is more than adequate," he pleaded.

Tears began to form in Dina Winters's eyes. Dina was her real name; I liked Daisy better. She sniffed a couple of times and caught herself. "You should be thinking about waterfront, Charlie, waterfront. You never lose with water. It just keeps appreciating."

Daisy wasn't that stupid. She had a brain but girlfriend was using her assets until she had him roped in.

"Why don't you both think about it and get back to me?" I said, flipping her another card. I had another appointment with clients coming in from New York who sounded like they were ready to buy, and I didn't need Daisy's waterworks holding me up.

My new business cards from Fabulous Shots were worth every dime of the two hundred dollars I'd conned Manny into spending. They really were fab-u-lous. Seventy-five dollars of his money had gone toward making me fifty pounds lighter, hollowing out my cheeks, and flattening my stomach. With a little erasing around the eyes I'd turned into one helluva guy magnet. I needed to make sure Quen got one of my cards.

"I really have to go," I said, looking at my watch. "I've got another client."

"Honey, let's not hold this lady up," Charlie who

was totally whipped said. "We took this long plane flight and we checked everything out on the web so why not just do it."

Daisy sniffed again. "I want you to think about water, Charlie. Can we call you tomorrow?"

"Sure you can."

Dina, Daisy, whatever, gave the apartment one last go around, Charlie trotting dutifully at her heels. By then I'd pretty much decided this Realtor business took a good deal of patience. Sure you could make big bucks if you bit your tongue and knew how to manipulate people. Biting my tongue was something I'd have to learn to do.

Finally Charlie and his eye candy left.

"How did it go?" Manny asked me when I returned to the office. I rolled my eyes and sucked in my breath. "That bad, huh?"

I explained what had happened. "That woman was still carrying on in the parking lot. I could hear her. She wanted Charlie to hold out for a villa."

Manny shrugged. "What do you care? If he buys her a waterfront place, that's more money in your pocket. Think commission, hon. Judging by their mode of transportation, old Charlie ain't hurting none. He can well afford to buy his trophy whatever she wants."

"I suppose."

"Speaking of which you want to have dinner with me sometime?"

I thought about it for a second. "Sure."

Hell I was hungry and Manny would buy me anything I wanted in reason, so I wouldn't shoot off my mouth to Lizzie about Sheena.

He made a good point, too, about the commission. The couple had shown up in a Hummer, one of those huge monstrous things in canary yellow that reminded me of a Brink's truck and cost a fortune.

"When's your next client?" Manny asked.

I squinted at the tiny wristwatch Jen had insisted I wear. She claimed I needed to look professional.

"They should be showing up any minute."

"You look nice," Manny said. "Not at all what I'm used to seeing you wearing."

Was he coming onto me? I glared at him. I hated the two-piece pant outfit. It wasn't me. The black slacks made me feel like a mortician and the long black cardigan that covered the sleeveless beige shell was hot and itchy. I had a double strand of fake pearls around my neck that were choking the daylights out of me. And on my feet were the ridiculous black pumps. My arches were already aching from all that standing.

I poured myself a glass of water when what I really wanted was a big ole glass of sweet tea, or a Biggie Size soda. In a pinch, water would have to do.

The etched glass doors of Flamingo Realty pushed open and two men walked in.

"Chere Adams please."

"Who wants to know?" I swear it slipped out. Truly it did. "I'm Chere," I admitted in my elocution voice and handed them my card "And you are?"

"Peter and Dustin Millard. Friends of Chet Rabinowitz and Harley Mancini's. They said to ask for you."

Walk-in's. I had the other appointment. I tossed a desperate look Manny's way hoping he would help me out, but my boss already had his sunglasses in hand, and was heading out of the door.

"You're in good hands with Chere," he said, looking over his shoulder and winking at me.

I started to wheeze. Stress always brings on my asthma. I made the two men sit, handed them some paperwork to fill out, then excused myself and went into the bathroom. I dug through my purse, found my inhaler and gave it a good squeeze. Wheeze. Wheeze. Wheeze.

Calm down, Chere. You can do this. You know you can.

When I came back Peter was gabbing on his cell phone. Judging from what I could hear of the one-sided conversation, he was talking to Chet.

"Yes, we're at Flamingo Realty. Yes, we got hold of Chere. You want to talk to her?"

Peter, who was the slenderer of the two held out the phone. "Chet wants to talk to you, hon."

By now I was breathing more normally. "Hey, Chet," I greeted in my best Realtor voice. "It was nice of you to send your friends."

He quickly gave me the scoop telling me that Peter and Dustin were brothers in from New York scouting out areas on Flamingo Row to start a business. One was gay and the other straight. They were in serious negotiations with Carlton Rogers about taking over the old liquor shop.

The store was in the historical district, otherwise known as "The Row" and right next door to Chet and Harley's flower shop. Now Peter and Dustin were talking about making the place a wine and cheese shop. Chet had been lobbying for a long time to get Carlton out, claiming his liquor store drew undesirables and scared off his customers.

Wine and cheese sounded too chi-chi to me. I liked Carlton's liquor store because he gave me endless credit and had what I wanted. It was also one of the few places carrying Colt these days, or at least admitted they did. And I liked my 45.

"Peter and Dustin Millard have plenty of money," Chet confided, lowering his voice. "Don't let them give you this crap about being restricted to a certain price range. One's a stockbroker, the other an attorney. Both earn easily high six figure salaries."

"Hmm." The cash register was ringing loudly in my ears. I repeated what Manny had said about me. "Your friends are in good hands."

My other clients who were locals still hadn't shown up and Peter and Dustin sounded like better prospects. The Houstons were actually Manny's clients, but he'd turned them over to me, and that made me suspicious. Manny wasn't that generous to begin with so there must be something up with them.

"What exactly are you looking for?" I asked, my slick Realtor smile in place. Damn it but the elastic waist of my pants were beginning to pinch and I hadn't eaten since breakfast, which was another tasteless boiled egg and a bowl of Special K.

This was my first day on the job and based on the people I'd been showing properties to, most didn't know what the hell they wanted. They were all on a mission to get something for nothing. Couldn't say I blamed them.

"Here's the thing," Dustin, who had to be the gay one, said expansively. "We don't plan to be here very often. We'll probably hire someone to run the business if we buy it. So we don't need much."

I eyeballed him. I can be quite intimidating thanks to my weight, especially when I draw myself up to my full height of five foot six. "Is it a studio you want to see?"

I thought about the renovations going on in the complex. There was a corner studio that one tenant wanted to unload. She was buying a house in town and needed money quickly. But two men in a studio; one as heavy as me, maybe heavier, lord help them, they'd be on top of each other.

Peter and Dustin exchanged looks. "Perhaps not a studio," Peter said, "Do you have a one bedroom? It doesn't have to face water. We're thinking of renting for short terms when we're not in town."

"I'll show you what I have," I quickly said, seeing another opportunity here. "Do you have financing?"

"Oh, yes we've been preapproved."

A big hurdle crossed. "Okay, let's see what's available." I grabbed my keys and whisked them out the door before they could think about returning another day.

Forty minutes later we were back in the sales and

leasing office. Peter and Dustin had taken photos of several apartments with a digital camera. They promised to be back in touch. After dealing with two clients in a row I was hungrier than a fat woman on a diet. And my client with the appointment still hadn't shown up.

I ushered the boys out the door and began rummaging through the briefcase, Jen's congratulatory present to me. I guess she felt guilty because she hadn't delivered on that cruise; the one she was probably taking Tre on for their honeymoon. It was unfair, I'd been the one who'd stuffed that box with her business cards, and he was an employee of WARP, the station sponsoring the raffle.

I'd just found my emergency supply of M&M's and a bag of stale chips when a woman's voice called from the door.

"Anyone there?"

Was I invisible? I'm not hard to miss and I was dressed like I was going to a funeral. What did she think? I was the cleaning lady? I shoved the M&M's and chips back in my briefcase and stomped to the front door. The back of my heels were really beginning to hurt. I probably had blisters. Four children, all roughly the same age, burst in through the door almost knocking me over.

"Whoa," I said, grabbing one of the girls by the arm. "Slow down. This ain't the Daytona racetrack you're on."

"Children have a lot of energy and need an outlet," the woman said briskly, as if it were no big deal that they were circling the place and sweeping papers off Manny's desk. "Healthy kids like to play."

"Not in here they don't. What can I do for you?"

I liked kids, even wanted a few, but mine were going to be disciplined.

A finger went up in the air, shutting me up. "My husband and in-laws will be right in. We'll talk to you then."

Snooty. Thought she was somebody and I wasn't.

Soon a puffed up man who seemed equally as arrogant as she, arrived with a bunch of people. I mean there were plenty of them. There was an older couple, and what must be their offspring and spouses. All together there had to be at least sixteen of them.

"The others decided to stay in the van," the red man said to his wife. Others? Don't tell me there were more. He shook his jowls at me expecting me to cower. "Where's Manny?"

I handed him a business card. "I'm in charge."

After glancing at my card, he tossed it aside. "I want Manny not you, Cherie."

"The name's Chere as in Sonny and Cher. Manny's not here and I'm not about to manufacture him. Who are you, anyway?"

"Thomas Houston. Mr. Houston to you. That there's Mrs. Houston and those are my children." He pointed to the obnoxious woman who'd arrived with the kids that were now whirling through the room like a tornado. They were totally out of control.

I was going to kill Manny when I got ahold of him. I was going to grab him by his little wiener and squeeze hard until it got big.

I didn't want to be rude because I didn't want to lose a job I had just started. So I said, "Because Manny said I should help you, I will."

"Help us do what?"

We were going around in circles and I was more than a little pissed. I didn't care about being professional.

"You're here to buy a condo, right?" Based on the size of that family they should be buying an entire building or two.

"We were looking to buy several condos but not from you."

There was something about me they didn't like. Well I didn't like them either. I was considering telling them to get the hell out of the sales office when a voice I recognized said.

"Hey, Tom, what seems to be the problem?"

Quen. He was standing in the doorway taking in the sight of me all puffed up, and those children skating across the floor and diving off my desk.

Thomas Houston on spotting Quen seemed to come down off his high horse.

"Hey Quen, old man, long time no see." They did one of those bear hugs that only men do. "I'd been expecting Manny to show me around not some chick. Now he's done a disappearing act."

So that was the problem. It wasn't my skin color that bothered him. It was me being female that was the problem.

"You look nice. Think you can help Tom and his family, sugar?" Quen said, entering the room and glaring at the out of control brats. "Okay, enough already, kids. Time to clean up. Get those papers off the floor. Get yourselves off the desk, and Randall since you're the oldest one, you make sure everyone gets this place in order. Now."

And just like that the madness ended. I could have thrown my arms around the man and kissed him. Then Quen turned to the Houston man and said, "Chere Adams is the best Realtor this town has.

She's a straight-up gal with a lot of smarts and she's handling two of my properties. If I were going to buy an apartment it would be from her."

How sweet is that? And you wonder why I had the hots for this man?

Chapter 5

"Five pounds, sugar. You've lost five pounds."

Quen high-fived me and I did a little mambo. I'd finally learned that move from step class, but it had taken me several classes to get it down.

Losing that weight felt good, having Quen's hands on me felt even better. I liked him touching me, moving an arm or leg into position as I struggled with a machine. Sometimes I struggled on purpose, and although his touching me could be considered part of his job; there were times I fantasized different.

I smiled into those chocolate eyes and tried not to lick my lips. I loved it that he called me sugar. Although weight loss and sweetener didn't go together, we were at least making progress. I was sick and tired of being called thick, and now that skinny Joya was coming to town I needed to get the weight off. She would be my incentive.

When you're busy like I'd been lately, you don't have time to eat properly. My meals had been candy bars and a bite or two of a sandwich here and there, but the weight was still disappearing. Jen said it was because I was exercising and on my feet showing real estate, and I wasn't just stuck behind a desk or laying on the couch watching mindless TV.

And now, after crawling out of yoga class at a ridiculous hour, Quen had waylaid me and insisted on a weigh-in. He handed me a power bar.

"Your reward," he said, sounding solemn. His eyes didn't have their usual sparkle.

"I thought you'd be excited for me. How come you're PMS'ing?" I quizzed, giving him a chicken neck, eyes popping.

"I am excited, sugar." One finger flicked my cheek playfully. He was treating me like his kid sister again and I'd better take it for what it was, or I'd be melting in a pool at his feet begging him to do me.

"Everyone should sound like you when they're happy."

"My ex is coming back to town, and it's kinda thrown me," he admitted.

"Holy Toledo! Joya's coming back?" I faked surprise. "I thought she'd had it with Flamingo Beach and we down-to-earth folks. What's she coming back for?"

Quen's smile seemed strained. "According to her grandmother, she burned out on the flight attendant job, took a leave of absence, and now needs to recuperate."

"So why did she choose here?"

He shrugged.

I didn't mean to sound sour but Joya's arrival was going to cause me grief. Plus it was going to put a kink in the plans I had for me and Quen. How could a girl my size compete with size two? In a small town like this I'd be sure to run into her even if we didn't move in the same circles.

"It'll be okay, sugar. It'll have to be." Quen chucked me under my chin and I got that warm fluttery feeling in my tummy.

He didn't know how big a crush I had on him, and how much I disliked it that Joya had shared his bed. Some said she'd really broken his heart. I was all for volunteering to repair that heart and make it whole again.

"I may have sold my first condo," I said excitedly. "Can I take you to dinner to celebrate?" I caught myself and added, "We can discuss renting your condos. There's all the paperwork to go over." I held my breath.

"You can take me anywhere you want, sugar, as long as it serves good healthy food." He chucked me under the chin again and began walking off. "Call me."

Quen had just given me the kind of opening I needed. I planned on calling him. Soon.

Later that evening, I couldn't open my apartment door no matter how much I jiggled my key. The stiff, stubborn lock refused to move and I kicked at the door in frustration.

"Open up you damn thing!"

I stalked down the hallway swearing and cussing. On top of everything else I was juggling, I now needed to call a locksmith to get into my place. The key had worked just fine this morning.

The door of an apartment creaked open. Shirley Babcock who had five children and no man in the house stuck her head out.

"The landlady was here," she announced.

"What do you mean, Shirley?" I asked. "Speak plainly now."

"She said you didn't pay your rent and she was going to lock your sorry ass out."

"She did not!" I bit back a stream of colorful cuss words. My back hit the wall of that hallway. I wanted to bang my head, have a temper tantrum and cry.

"What did she do with my stuff?" I asked.

Shirley's neck wobbled from one side to the other. "She said she was going to pitch it."

"She did not!"

Gawd! I couldn't let that happen. I had some expensive stuff in that apartment. My red leather sofa for one, and my antique glass table with the elephant feet and painted toenails; at least I thought it was antique. It cost me big money as did my zebra-skinned divan with the matching pillows where I watched my TV. My stereo was a Bose and my round bed, which was my pride and joy, was the kind that gyrated. I was still paying for them on time. I wasn't about to donate these items.

I dug into my purse, found my cell phone and stabbed at the landlady's programmed number. To hell with Mr. Cummings and his queen's English. This required plain old street language; ghettoese with a few well placed cuss words tossed in between. It was the only thing the ugly bitch would understand.

Wouldn't you know it? I got the bitch's answering machine. I left her a message and I gave her a certain time to get back to me. And just in case she didn't get it, I told her my posse would be coming to get my furniture one way or the other.

Shirley Babcock must have got me and so did the entire floor, because by the time the machine cut off Shirley's door was closed, and there wasn't a sound coming from any of the other apartments. No stereos, no people fussing, no babies crying. Nothing. Unusual, because in my building there was always a racket.

I pressed another button on my phone and waited.

"Yes, Chere," Jen greeted.

Thank God she at least answered. I explained my dilemma and waited, fingers crossed for what I hoped she would say.

"You can move into my apartment early if you want," she offered.

I made the sign of the cross and I wasn't Catholic. Now what was I going to do about clothes?

One thing at a time Chere. You have a roof over your head.

"Would you like me to come and get you?" Jen offered. Her niceness made me feel guilty. Here I was trying to get a promotion at the *Chronicle,* and ready to go over her head if she didn't come through.

"Nah, I can drive. I'm just so freaking mad."

She made these soothing noises meant to calm me down. I wasn't calm, hell who would be if everything you owned was in some woman's possession? And that included your full refrigerator with the ham, rack of ribs, frozen burgers and Dr. Peppers. That food wasn't cheap.

Burning rubber out of that parking lot, I made it over to Jen's place in record time.

As soon as she let me in, she handed me a spritzer; you know wine and water. I don't drink wine except when I'm trying to impress someone, but Jen wasn't a Colts kind of girl. In any case I especially appreciated the gesture.

She waited until we were seated on her sectional couch and I had shed a tear or two, before saying, "Your landlady can't just lock you out without arranging for you to pick up your things. You can take her to court you know."

"With what? I have no money. I'm hoping this deal with the Houstons goes through so that I can get my commission check and pay down some of my bills."

"File in small claims, it only requires a nominal fee. I'll lend you the money."

I shook my head. It was a sweet thing to offer.

"My things cost more than the allowable amount." There had to be another way.

"Okay, okay." She patted my shoulder awkwardly, "So what's the plan now?"

"Hope that I scared the living bejesus out of the witch, and she allows me access to the apartment."

"That would be good." Jen stood and handed me the apartment keys. "You know where everything is. If there's something you need you know where to find me. Just knock on 5B."

I remembered I didn't have clothes so I asked, "Think Tre will lend me a T-shirt and a pair of boxers so that I can get comfortable? And you think we can work out of here tomorrow so I don't have to launder a whole bunch of stuff?"

Jen squeezed my shoulder. "I can make both happen. Now you try to relax while I go find you something to wear."

She was back in half an hour with clothing draped over one arm. By then I had gone through her refrigerator eating everything and anything I could find. And there hadn't been much. I was beginning to realize there was a reason skinny people were skinny. What she had were the fixings for salad, a container with tuna fish and a plastic bag with pita. I was still starving.

Jen handed over a couple of Tre's T-shirts; the kind that had WARP written all over the front. Tre was the on-air personality for the radio station and made big bucks because they wanted to keep him. Now he had his own show which he and Jen co-hosted two nights a week, bringing down the house with the Jenna and D'Dawg show. The man was so whipped he'd even given her first billing.

"That's the best that I could do," she said, not adding that my caboose wouldn't fit into Tre's shorts

I thanked her and was thinking about underwear. I supposed I could hand wash what I was wearing and go comancho for one night, just until I could buy some tomorrow or that evil-assed woman let me into the apartment. There was no one here to see my fat bare ass except me.

"You don't look too good, Chere," Jen said giving me that compassionate stare, eyes slightly narrowed. "I'd be glad to stay the night and keep you company if you would like."

I didn't want no company. I wanted to be left alone to wallow in self pity and plan vengeance on my miserable land lady.

"No, no. I'll be okay. I'm going to take a shower, wash my underwear and change into a T-shirt."

Jen hesitated. What did she think I was going to

do, kill myself because some old broad had decided to lock me out of my apartment?

"I'll be fine," I insisted.

The minute she was out the door I turned on the television. Jen had one of those expensive wall units that fooled you into believing you were watching a movie on the big screen. Right now some skinny woman was on BET talking about the importance of good nutrition, and that America had a huge obesity problem. She was going on about what an undisciplined bunch we were. Over eating was an oral fixation she said, not that I exactly knew what that meant. When I think of oral, something totally different comes to mind.

Using the remote, I snapped off the television. Then I turned on the stereo and found a rap station. That was much better. When all you heard was thump, thump, thump, it didn't give you any reason to reflect.

I dragged my butt up the hallway and into Jen's bedroom, which was huge, almost the size of my apartment. It had French doors that led out to a balcony overlooking the boardwalk and gave a clear view of the ocean. The bed had fancy sheets on and a cover that matched the drapes at the windows. Well I'm not so sure they were drapes actually, they were material that dipped and curled, outlining the frame.

Right there in the middle of that room, in front of those French doors, I began taking off the clothes that I'd worn to the office. No one could see. I crossed the room to examine myself in the full length mirror to see if losing those five pounds made that much of a difference. My weight had always been my best friend. I trusted those folds and dimples more than any man. I'd been heavy for most of my life and truthfully it felt comfortable.

As a teenager I'd begun piling on the pounds, hoping that my appearance would protect me, especially when I started getting unwelcomed male attention. I'd been dumbfounded when the teenage boys that I'd known all of my life and played hide-and-seek with wanted to play an entirely different game. And when the neighbor's husband, who used to give me candy suggested that we play hide the eggplant and see what developed, I began to develop serious trust issues.

When I refused, he forced me to, threatening that he would tell my family I'd come on to him and was making him uncomfortable. This went on until I was sixteen and then one day when he whipped that old eggplant out I doused his thing with a plentiful amount of red pepper and that was that. From then on, boyfriend kept his distance.

Men! The majority are pigs; pigs with a one-track mind. And so I wallowed in my fat and pretended to be this happy, jolly woman with more confidence than most. But Ian Pendergrass who owned the *Chronicle* had seen how smart and vulnerable I was. It was he who'd given me an opportunity to better my life. But even Ian had expected something in return for being kind.

Now I was plain old wary of pretty much every man. For the most part I preferred it if they left me the hell alone; except for Quen. He was an old friend that I had this unexplainable thing for. Maybe it was because he never looked at me as if he wanted to toss me into bed. He treated me like his kid sister, nice comfortable Chere, easy to be around. I had mixed feelings about that. I wanted to be seen as a woman. His woman.

I was about to change that; starting with the dinner we two would have supposedly to discuss renting his apartments.

Crossing the white tile floor, I entered Jen's spotless bathroom. A huge, gilt mirror hung over the sink and I stared into it wondering if others saw me as I did. I didn't think of myself as particularly pretty. I had huge brown eyes and these double chins. What I'd always had was a great personality.

I walked over to the Jacuzzi tub. It was the kind you stepped down into and had big chrome knobs. Four large fluffy towels, a cool shade of mint, were folded in apricot-colored wicker baskets on the floor. Surrounding the tub were scented candles of various shapes and sizes. The woman must have quite the life.

I turned the water on full volume. Because it was a warm spring evening, the air conditioning hummed. I waited for the mirror to mist up before stepping under the shower and washing my underwear. I draped it over the sides of the tub and positioned my body under the jets. How long I stayed there I don't exactly know, but it must have been a while because when I finally turned that water off my bones no longer hurt. I wrapped my body into one of those mint towels. I was still hungry but in a far better mood. And now I had a plan.

I used one of Jen's expensive lotions to cream down my body then I tugged on Tre's shirt. Cell phone in hand I climbed onto Jen's big bed, pressed a button and called Sheena.

"I didn't expect to hear from you," she said.

"And why's that?"

"'Cause you're no friend. Friend's don't move in on another friend's man."

Sheena had no particular man that I knew of. Every man was her man.

"Come again," I said.

She got straight to the point. "Why you moving in on Manny?"

I kept forgetting how fast news travels in this town. But wait a minute, there'd been no one else around, so it had to be Manny who'd told her he saw me.

"Let's not forget Manny's dating Lizzie," I reminded her.

"Not for long. He'll soon be dating me."

"Of course, you're a ho," I wanted to say but I kept my mouth shut. I needed a favor so I sucked it up.

"You still friends with any of those boys from the hood?" I asked her.

"You mean Jerome and the Bloods?"

"Yep." I explained that I needed someone to shake my landlady up. "I just want them to scare the nasty witch a little and get real loud, that's all I'm asking."

"What's in it for me?" Sheena shot back.

"Manny is yours if you back off from Quen. He's got more money, anyway, and money is what you're after."

"Yeah, but Quen's finer and both men are professionals."

"You don't do professional," I said losing it. "Youse a ho."

Sheena sucked her teeth loudly. "You want a favor, you give me that new Coach bag you got for your birthday and I'll see what I can do."

"Fine. It's yours." I didn't like the damn bag anyway, but I knew it cost a lot of money. I'd pretended to like it because Jen had picked it out. She was trying to class me up, but brown isn't my color. My taste runs more to hot pinks. I like pizzazz, things that jump out at you. I wanted everyone to see me and know I was coming.

I hung up in her ear. Sheena would take care of it. She'd sell her own mother if there was something in it for her.

Later, I lay on Jen's sectional couch figuring out where to take Quen to dinner with my commission check that I was due. I was sick and tired of the Pink Flamingo; too many people that we knew plus that's where Jen always took me.

I thought about the new Flamingo Beach Spa and Resort. It should have fancy restaurants. There was also that steak and seafood place on the boardwalk, although in all my years of living in this town I'd never been there. I'd always wondered why anyone would call a restaurant the Flaming Flamingo? A gay bar I could see but a restaurant? The other option was the Catch All; a popular pick up joint, but this wasn't about being picked up. This was about having Quen notice me as a woman.

I must have fallen asleep and was dreaming. The next thing I knew someone was shaking me by the shoulders and I opened my eyes to a steady stream of sunlight.

"Quen?" I said sleepily.

"Not Quen, Jen."

"What time is it?"

"Nine o'clock. Time to go to work."

It couldn't be. I scrambled up. "Holy Toledo." I'd missed my workout session. Now I'd have hell to pay.

As confirmation of that, my cell phone rang.

It didn't take a rocket scientist to figure out who was on the other end of the line.

I debated whether or not to pick up. Finally my conscience got the better of me and I reached for it.

"Let it ring," Jen said, stopping me.

"What if it's Quen?"

"You can call him back on your time. We have work to do."

She dropped a stack of letters next to me. "Some of these are a month old. Now go brush your teeth. Later you can make nice."

Rolling my eyes I hurried off.

Chapter 6

Much as it aggravated me to let the phone ring. I thought it might be a good thing. Let Quen wonder why I hadn't shown up.

I hurried into the bathroom and took a quick shower. Then I put on my still-damp underwear which I'd forgotten to toss in Jen's dryer. When I was through I scrambled back into yesterday's clothing.

Jen had coffee going. She handed me a cup and I sipped slowly waiting to wake up. "You want toast?" she asked.

It was all she was offering so I nodded. My

stomach was making funny little noises and if I didn't eat something I would probably pass out.

I climbed onto a stool at the counter and watched her put that dry toast on a plate.

"You got butter?" I asked

"If you're on a diet you shouldn't."

Dry toast. Yuk! Disgusting. But it was better than nothing. I gobbled that tasteless meal down like it was porterhouse steak.

A couple of hours later Jen allowed me to take a break from my reading. By then I was hallucinating so badly that the golden arches of McDonald's wobbled before my eyes. I would do just about anything for a double whopper, fries and a vanilla shake. Dang if that woman didn't have ESP.

"Ten minutes," Jen warned. "That should give you just enough time to go to the bathroom and return Quen's call then it's back to work we go."

Grabbing my cell phone I made a beeline for her balcony. She didn't need to hear me talking to him. I checked my messages because I'd left my phone on vibe. Sure enough Quen had left me two. On the last one he'd forgotten to call me "sugar." That must mean I was in real trouble.

Manny had left a message and so had Sheena.

Since I didn't have time to return all four calls I had to decide which was important.

Okay, getting my stuff back was top of the list. And I really should find out if Sheena had gotten hold of the Bloods. On the other hand, hearing Quen's voice would make me feel good, and I did owe him an explanation even though he was probably calling to ream me out. Manny must want me to come into work. Initially our agreement had been for weekends but he was relying on me more and more. So what had started out as part-time was quickly becoming full-time. Tonight I had my elocution class. Mr. Cummings was a tough SOB if you missed two classes consider yourself booted.

Now what to do?

"Chere, you've got seven minutes," Jen called from inside the apartment. I had to make at least one call and I needed to use the bathroom.

I dialed into voice mail and got Sheena's message. She'd come through for me. I guess she wanted that Coach purse badly. When I stabbed the return call button her phone rang and rang until finally voice mail picked up. I left a message.

"Thanks for taking care of that piece of business," I said. "I'll call the nasty witch and make arrangements to come by the apartment with a moving truck. Tell Jerome and the Bloods I owe them."

After I disconnected I stabbed another button and returned Quen's call.

"I was worried," he said the minute he recognized my voice. "What happened to you?"

"I'm sorry I overslept."

I told Quen that I'd gotten locked out of my apartment and how the stress had caused me to oversleep.

"Not good," he said. "But listen I can't afford for you to miss another session. It cost me money when these things happen." He was being nice but I could tell he was ticked. "Can you make up the time this evening?"

"I can't," I explained. "I have elocution class. If I don't show up Mr. Cummings might boot me out."

"Who's that?"

"He's my teacher."

"Chere. You have two minutes. Time to wrap it up," Jen called from inside.

I ended the call and told him I'd be there tomorrow. Then I called Manny. He sounded professional. I could tell by his tone he was with a client.

"I called before because the deal with the Houstons looks pretty good. I don't know how you managed it. They've been procrastinating for a year and driving me crazy. Anyway, there financing is set and now they're pushing hard for a quick closing. The three units are vacant so the process should be relatively easy. I'll be there with you every step of the way."

I'm sure he would looking for his piece of the action.

"Alls I'm interested in is collecting my commission check. Those people were damn difficult," I said. I was sure the only reason they'd made an offer was because the husband got along with Quen.

But a sale was a sale and I was desperate. I had the unexpected expenses of the moving truck and I had to pay for storage space. I'd have to pay back-rent to my witch of a landlady who was threatening to take me to court. Plus I had to come up with the five hundred dollars Jen wanted for her place. Hell, I was damn near close to destitute.

"Chere your ten minutes are up," Jen snapped.

"I'll be right there."

"I'll try to get to you before elocution class," I said to Manny then I hung up.

Two weeks later, and fifty cents left in my purse, I was at my first closing. The Houston's sat at one end of the table and my weasel of a boss, Manny, was at my side. Thank God, the Houston's children had been left home. I'd actually hoped to see the little buggers mischievous as they were. Must be my biological clock ticking.

Manny kept grumbling that he should be getting a bigger cut of the commission. The Houstons had been his clients first and he'd done me a favor by handing them off to me. I wanted to slap him. Did he think I was a fool if he thought they'd end up buying he would never have given them to me.

I sweated through the entire closing. The Houstons had brought their attorney with them and he'd examined every piece of paperwork and made sure every *i* was dotted and *t* crossed. I hung in, managing to keep smiling. At the end of it I would get my reward. I needed that check.

Six percent of three units. That would be more money than I'd seen in my lifetime. It would more than make up for the last two weeks of doing without and the pleading and groveling. I'd had to postdate the landlady's rent check, because whether or not the boys had scared her, she wanted money in hand. My things were being held hostage and I'd paid too much for my furniture to donate it to her.

I'd had to postdate Jen's rent check as well, but at least she was understanding. I loved her building, especially the view. Everyone was nice except for that meddling cow Camille Lewis. People's eyes literally popped out of their heads when I proudly announced I lived at 411 Flamingo Place.

The last piece of paper was signed and we shook hands. The Houstons were now acting as if I was the best thing they'd encountered since rye bread. And I was smiling from ear to ear, thinking, "check, check, check I'm in the money."

"Congratulations, we did it," Manny said, high-fiving me the moment they'd left. He zoomed in for a kiss while trying to cop a feel at the same time. "Eeeek! You're getting skinny." His hand squeezed my butt. I swatted him away. By the hungry look in his eye he was on a mission. "Let's celebrate over dinner."

No way. I had other things to do. I'd lost ten pounds and one dress size. It felt good saying I had other plans and actually meaning it.

I was meeting Quen to celebrate this sale, my first one. We needed to talk about his properties and what he wanted to do with them.

"Touch base with me tomorrow," Manny said, "I've been talking with an out of state client who's looking for a rental. She'll sign the lease without seeing the actual space. I just need to shoot her a couple of photos of the property."

"I will."

I left thinking that I needed to find a place to change clothes and touch up my makeup. I suppose I could use the office bathroom but I didn't trust Manny not to just walk in. The only option was my old Honda.

Quen and I had agreed to meet at this new Indian restaurant he suggested. The place specialized in vegetarian dishes and that was new to me. Quen had offered to pick me up and he'd made it sound like a real date. I'd declined, telling him I didn't know how long the closing would take.

Hopefully Taj, the new restaurant, offered something more than rabbit food. I was sick to death of salads and would die for a spoonful of mashed potatoes and a juicy pork chop. But it was my dime we were spending so I should get to eat what I want.

Taj was located smack in the middle of Flamingo Row. It was owned by a white guy with a turban and fake accent. He claimed to have spent time in India and was smart enough to know that his location on Historical Row would draw tourists; lots of them.

The local population when they went out to eat wanted a solid plate of food. And that's why the chicken-and-rib joints were jumping. They gave you a good-size dish and didn't cost a fortune.

I sat in the car, stretched my legs out and ditched

the panty hose. I had my blouse halfway over my head when a thumping on the car window damn near scared me to death. I tried yanking down the blouse but it got stuck on a layer of fat on my middle. In frustration I pulled the thing over my head and turned to glare at the person. I didn't care if they saw my triple D cups. As far as I was concerned I had on more clothes than three quarters of the population.

"What do you want, Manny?" I barked when I spotted the weasel.

"You forgot this," he said, waving an envelope at me while practically dribbling.

In my rush to leave I'd forgotten my check. I needed that money to pay for dinner. I'd planned on pulling into the first check cashing place I saw and happily paying the percentage they charged. I rolled down the Honda's window and grabbed the envelope.

"Don't you be spying on me!" I yelled.

Poor Manny he couldn't pull his eyes away from my boobs. "I'm not spying on you," he said. "I'm just here to give you your money."

I thanked him and rolled up the window. After Manny had gone back to wherever he came from, I shoved my large butt into a pair of black pants and pulled a sleeveless black tunic top, the kind that covered your butt, over my head. I missed my bright colors. I had a red scarf still tied around my neck and I made a belt of it. Luckily it fit.

I glanced in the rearview mirror and made a face. All that sweating had my makeup running. I found a tissue and swatted my face. Then I put on blush, eyeliner and mascara and added a slash of red to my lips. A spritz of the perfume I'd helped myself to from Jen's desk, and I was done. I was going to be late and I still needed to cash that check.

A half an hour later I managed to find a parking spot on a side street off Historical Row. The Row is a people-friendly street that doesn't allow cars. I'd already called the restaurant and asked the person who answered to let Quen know that I was running late. Hopefully he got the message.

The turban-headed fool who owned Taj stood out front at the entrance greeting people. He stood next to a big ceramic elephant and the elephant truthfully looked better than him.

"Do you have a reservation?" he asked me as if I smelled.

"As a matter of fact I do." I swept by him and entered a little courtyard with about a dozen tables. A bunch of potted palms had white lights on them. I still didn't see Quen.

"Can we get you seated?" the owner asked, on my heels, breathing down my neck. He was acting as if he expected me to steal the stuff on the tables.

"I'm meeting somebody," I tossed over my shoulder and, waddled into the darkened interior with more flickering lights, except these were candles. There was a strong smell of incense everywhere.

"Over here, sugar," Quen's voice called from a dark corner.

He straightened to his full height of six foot four and my breath caught in my throat. By the light of the illuminating candles I caught a glimpse of a green polo shirt, the kind with the fancy logo, and tan slacks. The material of that shirt was stretched tight across his broad chest. Dark hairs escaped the two little buttons opened at his throat. Dang the man was fine.

Quen had chosen a table on the other side of another ceramic elephant. At first I thought maybe he didn't want to be seen with me. A man who looked like Quen had to have plenty of action. Discreet action; look at the number of women he trained; and most of them didn't look like me, many were skinny as a rail. I got over putting myself down really quick when he approached and took my hand, giving it a little squeeze.

"This is the lady I was waiting for," he said to the

owner. "Isn't she just about the finest thing you've ever seen?"

Turban head cleared his throat and nodded in agreement. He must know who was paying the bill.

In front of all the diners Quen kissed my cheek. My knees knocked so hard I thought I would fall and my heart jumped a hurdle. Quen was coming around and recognizing that I had sex appeal. Manny Varela obviously thought I did, and so did Dickie Dyson of Dyson Luxury Limousines. Chumps that they both were.

With all those people staring, I followed Quen to our table. It was a lucky thing he had a good grip on my hand.

When we were seated he said, "Baby girl, you are looking good."

I wasn't sure how to take that. I mean he'd seen me just yesterday for one of our sessions. When he reached over and stroked my bare arm I shivered.

"Cold?"

"Not at all."

"So why are you trembling?"

He'd noticed. He made a muscle with my arm. "Just look at that. You are getting toned."

Quen's open admiration was just the incentive I needed. He was acting like I was pita and I'd only lost ten pounds. What would happen when I was down fifty? Would he jump my bones? Wishful thinking on a girl's part.

An Indian waiter was lurking about trying to be invisible. Quen turned over the drink menu, glanced at it and handed it to him. "We're just having water, right?"

"Right." I could use a beer but didn't need the lecture.

When the waiter left I stuck my nose in the regular food menu and didn't recognize a thing. "What would you recommend?"

"Everything. It's all good and freshly made."

Quen began telling me about the various dishes and the ingredients that went into making them. None of them sounded particularly appealing but I listened, pretending to be interested. I even managed to sound smart, tossing in a question or two about calories and cholesterol counts, not that I've ever paid much attention. I was just happy to be with Quen and in my head I was thinking about what our children would look like.

We picked our meals and Quen placed the order. While we waited to be served I brought up the subject of his two apartments.

"What do you think about multiple listing?" I asked. "You want those apartments moved quickly, right?"

"Right on, sugar. Keeping them empty is costing me a fortune."

"I'll get them rented for you," I promised, and I meant every word. I was going to get those condos rented if it killed me.

With all those candles flickering, low music in the background and intimate conversation around me, I was starting to feel like we were on a real date. And because I really liked Quen, I needed to know about the competition.

"So when is Joya coming back?" I asked carefully.

I noticed the muscle in his jaw jump but otherwise there was no change in expression.

"Granny J tells me it should be any day now. She and I get along. She knew how cut up I was when the marriage ended so she went out of her way to warn me of Joya's coming."

"That was nice of her. I would think she'd be on her granddaughter's side."

"Granny J's never taken sides. That's why I like her. She's always been fair."

"How long were you two married?"

"Me and Granny J?"

"Don't play with me."

"A little less than five years," Quen said. "Joya and I were very young."

"How young?"

"She was nineteen and I was twenty-one."

"That's young. So how come you got married that young?"

"I'll tell you after we eat."

I didn't know anything about their marriage. I'd just moved from the Bronx when they were breaking up. Flamingo Beach had been buzzing with the gossip. You'd think no one had ever gotten divorced before and Joya was being called some pretty rotten names.

Our food arrived. After the waiter left Quen whisked off the covers. He'd ordered some kind of bean dish he called dahl and I'd ordered mulligatawny soup though I could barely pronounce it. And I'd ordered a fish dish with plenty of rice. Much as I hated to admit it everything smelled delicious. But maybe it had something to do with me starving.

Reluctant to let Quen off the hook, I returned to the conversation. "So you were telling me why you got married young."

Quen set his knife and fork aside. "Because I had to. Because it was the right thing to do."

I wasn't sure how to interpret that so I did in the only manner I understood.

"Shotgun wedding?"

"Something like that."

"And you did the right thing. Nobody gets married because someone gets pregnant in this day and age. So how come you did?"

There was a gleam in Quen's eyes. "You're asking some mighty personal questions, sugar."

"Am I? It's not like I'm a stranger. I was there for that breakup but you never ever talked about it, never once said a word."

I didn't think I was overstepping. Quen and I had met at the Haul Out in the midst of that mess. He'd be sitting at the bar, nursing a beer when I toddled in. He'd looking lonely and pathetic like he needed rescuing. I struck up a conversation with him but couldn't get more than a one word sentence out of him. I blamed my fat for his lack of interest in me. But truthfully he wasn't interested in anyone. He was suffering from a broken heart.

There had been speculation and rumors. Some said Joya had cheated on him; others said she'd married him then refused to go to work and that she'd set herself up for alimony. All I knew was that Quen was moping around. And then out of the blue he'd decided to go back to school and become a nutritionist.

Quen reached across the table and took my hand.

"Don't get mad at me, babe. There are things a fellow just can't talk about. Let's just say Joya and I were young and really didn't know each other."

I spooned rice in my mouth and sucked on it like it was ice cream. I was that hungry. "How do you feel about her coming back to town? It must feel funny."

"I'm just trying not to think about it."

He might not want to talk but I needed an answer to a particular question.

"Do you still love Joya?" I asked, holding my breath.

Quen looked at me with those soulful brown eyes of his, the tendons at the sides of his neck pulsed. After a while he said, "Joya will always have a special place in my heart."

And with that my hopes of getting this man interested in me were dashed. No way could I compete with Joya Hamill unless she'd changed drastically over the last five years.

And even so, she'd have to have grown buckteeth and a tail.

Chapter 7

I was lounging poolside at 411 Flamingo Place when my cell phone rang. Flopping onto my back, I reached for the rattan purse that I'd stuffed everything into: book, extra pair of sunglasses, bottled water, sunblock and a spare candy bar or two in case I got hungry.

"Yeah," I drawled, shoving my sunglasses onto my head to get a better view of the man in a Speedo on the diving board. Only a brave, confident man wore those tiny bathing suits that left nothing to the imagination.

"I rented one of your apartments," Manny said,

sounding totally pleased with himself. "Now you and me can have dinner."

I ignored the last part and managed to crawl into a seated position. "You rented Quen's apartment?"

"Yes, to Emilie Woodward—the woman in charge of leisure sales at the Flamingo Beach Spa and Resort. She didn't even try to bargain when I told her what the price was."

"Excellent. I love you, Manny." The words just sort of popped out, and for that brief second I meant them. Quen was going to be pleased.

I would have to split my commission with Manny but I was still excited. That meant one down and only one more to go. Juggling two jobs was starting to wear me out. I'd never worked so hard in my life, and I planned on kicking back today since it was my first day off in what seemed like years. Today was going to be all about me I decided.

Earlier I'd taken the time to wander around Jen's complex cataloguing everything it had to offer. And there had been quite a bit. The main floor where the lobby was, offered all types of services: everything from banking, dry cleaning, a mini grocery store and a coffee shop.

The gym I knew about because it was where I worked out. But outdoors there were also tennis and handball courts plus a jogging track that ran adjacent to the boardwalk. When you were taking a run you could see the ocean. There was also a small barbeque area with picnic tables, and there were hot tubs throughout the grounds and another pool.

Talk about living large. I'd never quite experienced anything like it.

"Now that I've taken care of this for you, don't you think I deserve something special?" Manny, the shameless dog, asked.

I sat up straight and began laughing. Mr. Speedo was jumping up and down on the diving board. After posing several times like Mr. Universe, he dove into the pool and in the process that teeny, weeny bathing suit slipped and something went flying out of the front, a sock maybe? The residents, sunning, were laughing so hard it became almost impossible to hear Manny.

"What did I say that was so funny?" Manny sounded annoyed.

"Nothing. I just saw something that reminded me of you."

I laughed again because Mr. Speedo's weenie was even smaller than Manny's. Imagine that? I started laughing again.

Manny's voice came through the earpiece. "How come you can go out with Quen Abrahams but you can't go out with me?" he whined. "I make more money. I can buy you things."

"It isn't always about money," I replied. Probably the whole town had seen me and Quen at Taj and put their own spin on it.

I thanked Manny for renting the apartment and before I hung up I asked, "When does the Woodward woman want to move in?"

"As soon as she can. She's a transplant, here because the hotel made her an offer she couldn't refuse and she's sick of living on the premises."

"She's that anxious? I'd be happy if anyone let me live anywhere for free."

"Not if you can't ever get away from work."

"I'll discuss the rental with Quen," I said and hung up. Then I propped myself up on my elbows and watched Mr. Universe try to make a dignified exit. But everyone was staring at him and laughing so hard their sides ached.

A woman sat down heavily on the lounge chair next to me. She carried a cell phone and wore dark glasses.

"Hello," she said. "Nice day for the pool."

I smiled back at her until I recognized it was Camille Lewis. She gulped down her ice tea and I waited.

"You moved into 5C," Camille said knowingly.

"Are you renting or staying for free until you can find a place?"

It was none of her business so I didn't answer.

"We're next door neighbors, Camille Lewis, remember? I live across the hall in 5D."

"Umm, hmm."

I'd avoided her like the plague because I knew her mouth had no cover. I'd seen her coming down the hallway a couple of times and hid.

I flopped onto my chest and closed my eyes, pretending to go to sleep.

Something ice cold ran the length of my spine and I rolled over.

"What the hell …"

"Hey, sugar," Quen said. "I didn't expect to find you out catching some rays."

My tongue felt heavy and my stomach fluttered. The man was a walking talking billboard for sex. His muscles rippled and his ebony skin shone; oiled and sweaty he glistened under the afternoon sun.

I couldn't take my eyes off his body. How was it possible for anyone not to have a spare ounce of flesh on him? I was used to seeing Quen in shorts and a T-shirt not bare chested, wearing swimming trunks that stopped midthigh. Now all I could think about was jumping his bones and the fact that it might have been a mistake to wear a bikini when you had as many rolls of flesh as I did.

"Hey, Quen," Camille Lewis said, leaning into us. She acted as if they were the best of friends.

I sat upright positioning my towel over my bulging middle. Quen was not alone, a bunch of skinny groupies trailed him; at least I assumed they were groupies. There were four of them, an entire United Nations. One was Asian, the other Latino, and the other Caucasian. The last, wearing a thong that barely covered her privates, was African American. All were rail-thin and well proportioned. I despised them on sight especially since they were staring at me as if I were a beached whale.

But at least I knew my boobs were real and not pumped up with some filler. I forgot about my tummy and sat up straight, sticking my 40 triple Ds practically in Quen's face.

"We've got good news, babe," I said.

You should have seen the Latino woman's face as she tried to figure out what was going down.

"I could use good news, sugar." Quen dropped down onto a spare lounger next to me. The four women remained standing unsure what to do next. Quen waved them off.

"Catch up with you ladies later. Chere and I need to talk."

Quen picked up my bottle of sunscreen and poured it in his palms. He began rubbing my arms and legs. A delicious scent of oranges filled my nostrils and it wasn't my sunscreen causing that smell. It took everything I had not to throw my arms around his neck and let him feel the crush of a woman with real flesh.

Camille Lewis, sick of being ignored had gotten up and walked away. She was on the far side of the pool keeping an eye on us while yakking on her cell phone. I took a deep breath so as to clear my head and repeated what Manny had told me.

Right in front of all of those people, Quen leaned over and laid one right on me. It was a big smackaroo right on the lips, and it left me cross-eyed and feeling as if I was floating. Things around me were moving in slow motion and wavering in and out.

"That's for renting my apartment," he said.

"And I'll rent the other soon," I promised, when I was able to catch my breath.

Quen continued to massage liquid into my flesh. His touch left me aching to get out of that suit. "I want to talk to you about something else," he said.

"I'm listening."

Quen's smile, a flash of white against black, left me breathless.

"How would you feel about being on the D'Dawg show?"

I bolted upright and clutched that towel to me. "Me! I don't have anything to say."

"Sure you do. You're my poster child. D'Dawg's invited me on to promote my nutritionist business. This is huge. I can't turn down free publicity. So I was thinking if you and I partnered it might make it more interesting for the listening audience."

"What would we tell them?"

"Well I could talk about our exercise program, and that eating right combined with healthy exercise helps burn calories. I could discuss menu plans guaranteed to make people lose weight. You'd be my walking, talking example of a person who's followed my plan and seen results."

Heaven help me if he knew I was cheating on his diet.

"I can go you one better," I said.

"Talk to me, sugar."

"How about you prepare meals for me. I mean you cooked them from scratch. You can cook, can't you?"

Smiling, he nodded. "My momma raised a full-service brotha."

"Okay. So we go on the talk show and I tell the peoples that I went to you for help because I wanted to lose weight. Then I tell them we work out together, and you designed a menu plan exclusively for me, and that you can do the same for them. We talk about how much weight I've lost and how under your supervision I'll lose even more. We set it up so that we'll be back on the program to discuss my progress in a few weeks."

"You're a genius," Quen said. "I'd be like that Jenny woman."

"Yeah, she makes big bucks, and I'll be your spokesperson. I can be Kirstie or Fergie. Name it."

"How about just being Chere?" Quen kissed me on the lips again; a nice juicy one. By then I was so hot I wanted to dive into the deep end of that pool. I could feel everyone looking, especially the women. They were all probably wondering what I had and they didn't. I just knew Camille's phone had to be smoking.

I knew how to be Chere. She was comfortable. What I didn't know how to be was one of those skinny-minny high-maintenance women.

Quen now spoke as if he was talking to himself. "And if I cook up these dishes and feed them to you, we can figure out what works and what doesn't. So who's buying the groceries, me or you?" He chuckled.

I cut my eyes at him. "Me, of course."

"When should we start?"

"This evening." Hey, my mother didn't give birth to no fool, jump on opportunity when it's there.

"Let's shoot for tomorrow. How about you come to my place?" Quen stood and stretched. "Tonight I have dinner plans."

I wanted to scream, "With who?" By then those rippling muscles had me close to orgasmic. Like a horny dog my tongue practically hung out as I watched him strut away. Lucky woman whoever she was.

The minute Quen was out of range, Camille swooped down like a vulture. She was still clutching that damn cell phone.

"You two have something going?"

"We're friends." I rolled over onto my stomach and closed my eyes again.

"Define friends. I saw him kiss you."

"Read into it what you want." I made my voice sound groggy and bit my tongue. What I really wanted to tell her was to stuff the cell phone where the sun don't shine.

Camille sucked her teeth. "Lucky that I like you.

That's why I'm telling you this. That man has plenty of women so you may not want to take him seriously."

"And that's supposed to have me worried?"

I wished she would leave me the hell alone. All I wanted to do was close my eyes and think about Quen's kisses. That and the meals he was going to cook for me. I didn't need Camille messing with my fantasies.

"I'd be," Camille said. "Take a look at you and take a look at him."

With that she walked away. Nasty bitch!

Later, I was seated in a chair at the beauty shop where everybody went to get their hair done; everyone in town who was black, anyway. I'd decided it was time to get the weave off. It was costing me too much money in maintenance and Jen said it made me look heavier.

La Veronique the woman who'd done my hair for years was cutting the weave out.

"What you looking to get, hon?" she asked.

I stabbed a flamingo-colored acrylic nail at a picture in the magazine I was flipping through. "What about this?"

"Nah, that ain't you." La Veronique snapped her gum. "Pick another."

I stabbed at another photo. "This is me."

The model had the Missy Elliott thing going on, tendrils of hair partially covering one eye.

"You can't pull that off," La Veronique said. "You need to be realistic."

Shoot. And so it went. Ten minutes later we settled on something that worked for both of us but La Veronique thought I should color my hair blonde. I thought about it for a moment, and was actually tempted, then I shook my head. I needed to keep it professional.

"I got this new job. Clients might be put off," I said.

"People wasn't put off by Shari Belafonte. Why should they be put off by you?"

"Shari can pull it off. I might not be able to." Now that's realism for you.

My self confidence was beginning to take a beating. I'd never before set my sights on men like Quen and the truth was I still wasn't sure how to read him. He seemed to go for the slim, classy types, like his ex-wife, Joya, and the women I had seen trailing him earlier today; women with perfect bodies and perfect faces. Face it, I had neither.

I'd gotten used to the way that I looked, but now I felt lacking. It might have something to do with volunteering to be the spokesperson for Quen's nutrition business. If I was going to be in the public eye I didn't want to look like no freak, and I didn't want people feeling sorry for me.

"Let's stick to dark brown," I told La Veronique. "You can throw in highlights or something."

"You sure?"

"Sure as my name is Chere."

Then I sat back and let her do her thing.

Around me hair dryers droned, and fragrances of frying oil mingled with hairspray. There was the usual smell of burning hair coming from hot combs and curling irons. I tuned into the conversations around me. If you wanted to know anything, the Curl and Weave was the place to go and served multiple purposes. While getting your hair done the stylist listened to your woes, and anyone who had a worse story than yours put their two cents in. Call it cheap therapy for black folks.

One woman was having problems with her husband and was threatening to do in the "ho" that kept him out late at night. I prayed that "ho" wasn't Sheena because the woman truly sounded like she meant business. Somebody else was going on about the upcoming centennial. In a year or so Flamingo Beach would be celebrating it's one hundredth birthday. Preparations were already underway, new buildings were being constructed, and revitalization efforts had begun on Flamingo Row.

"The city commissioned an artist from Miami to make 100 flamingos," someone else said. "They're to be placed all over town and then put up for auction. The proceeds go to the beautification of our town."

This was all news to me. I'd read somewhere about other cities doing a similar thing with cows and pigs, but flamingos? Oh, well.

A loud voice mentioned Joya Hamill's name and I really tuned in.

When I looked in that direction I spotted Joya's grandmother, owner of Joya's quilts, seated under the dryer. She was conducting a loud conversation with the woman next to her who was equally as old, if not older. She was the only white woman in the place. I recognized Ida Rosenstein because she lived on Jen's floor. The old lady was hard of hearing, and as she so often said it, "color blind." Ida didn't care whether you were black, white or purple.

"So when is your granddaughter coming home?" she asked

"Any day now," Granny J answered. "As soon as she can straighten a few things out."

"What does she have to straighten?" Ida asked, dipping a head covered in rollers out from under the dryer.

"You know young people," Granny J said. "She found an apartment here, and now it's just a matter of making sure her leave from work comes through. Then she'll pack up her things and get a stand-by ticket. You know she works for the airlines."

"Why did you say she was moving back?" Ida asked. "I thought she liked her stewardess job?"

I was totally tuned in. I didn't want to miss a word.

"Keep your damn head still—" La Veronique warned "—or I'll hurt you."

Granny J got kind of quiet which meant I really had to strain my ears. "Joya's just coming home for a while. She finds the flight attendant job stressful and she says the glamour's gone. Now you've got to keep an eye out for terrorists and they have them cleaning up the plane. She's sick of cutbacks and people complaining."

"Hmm!" Ida snorted. "Her coming home wouldn't have anything to do with that muscle-bound jerk she was married to?"

Jerk? Where did the old witch get off calling my man a jerk? Quen had never been a jerk as far as I knew. Big he might be but mean he was not. I should have given that busybody a piece of my mind. Instead I sucked in a mouthful of hot air and waited for Granny J's answer.

Snip. Snip. Snap. Snap. La Veronique laid down her scissors and began greasing my scalp, prepping it for the harsh relaxer. She was tuned in, as was the rest of the shop, and at the volume those two old ladies were going at, you'd be deaf not to miss it.

"You know," Granny J said, sounding a little sad, "it's hard to tell young people anything today. I thought Quen was good for Joya. He settled her down."

"Maybe she didn't want to be settled. Maybe that's exactly why she left him," Ida said wisely. "And maybe now she's changed her mind."

Except for the droning dryers, the shop was now suspiciously quiet. It sounded to me like Ida might be onto something.

Could Joya Hamill-Abrahams be coming back to town to pick up where she left off with Quen?

It would be a cold day in Flamingo Beach before I let that happen.

Chapter 8

"Come on in and have a seat." Luis Gomez, editor in chief of the *Flamingo Beach Chronicle* said, waving his stinky unlit cigar at me. As I entered "The Dungeon"—his hole of an office, he moved a stack of papers from one chair to another.

"What can I do for you?" Luis peered at me over his half moon glasses. "There's something different about you. New hair, makeup, dress?"

Typical man he didn't have a clue.

"I lost fifteen pounds," I said proudly.

"Hmm. How did you do that?"

"The usual way. Diet. Exercise."

Luis was making conversation. He really didn't want to hear how I lost weight so I spared him the details. Plus Luis was a little scared of me because he knew I knew his boss, Ian, and in a more intimate way.

"Let me just get to the point," I said, sensing I was losing him quickly.

Luis's eyes darted back to his monitor. I could tell his mind was on other things and not on me. I'd had to beg and plead with Lola, his lazy-ass assistant to get in to see him. I'd even had to buy the bitch lunch and then she agreed to squeeze me in, and then she wanted to know what this was all about.

"Sure, go ahead. I'm listening."

The hell he was. But I had to be real careful about how I positioned this so I didn't sound disloyal. And so I approached it in the only style I knew, real straightforward.

"It's like this," I said. "I'm here to ask for a raise because I deserve it."

"Think so?" Luis smiled at me as if we were sharing an off-color joke.

"I've been working here three years and during that time I've had three bosses. Who do you think keeps them on track?"

Luis crossed his fingers under his chin and gave me his full attention.

"Well there's something to be said for longevity, and you are well informed."

"Pays to keep up. Plus I read every damn letter the *Dear Jenna* column gets—" damn had slipped out "—and I give my opinion."

"And your point being?"

I puffed out my chest. Luis eyes were now stuck on my triple Ds. Ah ha I had him!

"My point being that not only do I deserve a raise but I deserve to have my name mentioned in the column."

Luis lips twitched. He thought it was funny. We'd see who had the last laugh.

"And how would you suggest I break the news to your boss. Should I tell her that her column is now a joint venture and needs to be renamed?"

I took a deep breath. "I'm just saying give credit where credit is due. And yes I've come up with a name, *Breaking it down with Chere and Jenna.*"

If a deejay like Tre Monroe could step down off his high horse, and share a couple of shows with his fiancé and even change the show's name so she got recognition then Luis could do the same for me. I'd been here for Jen, stuck with her through all sorts of garbage. I was loyal.

She's been loyal to you, too. She's letting you rent an apartment she could get four times more for at five hundred dollars per month. She's kicking in the rest.

Luis threw back his head and roared. I didn't know what was so funny.

His skinny ass assistant, Lola, stuck her head in the doorway. "Are you okay Mr. Gomez. Would you like me to get you some water?"

Lola didn't offer me water. I wasn't worth her time. She knew who provided a paycheck. Luis looked at me again and began to sputter. What the hell was so funny?

After awhile I figured better join him and we laughed together. Then Luis picked up the phone and pushed a button. How rude I thought.

"Jen," he said. "Can you come into my office for a minute. Chere's in here with me and we need to include you."

Busted! I wasn't sure how this was going to go over. I mean I was seated in her boss's office and it must look like I was complaining and had gone clear over her head. But it wasn't as if I hadn't brought up the topic of a raise and recognition before.

She'd ignored me and I had to do something. This

was about money and recognition, and me being able to live in the manner I could easily become accustomed to. I wasn't going to get rich on real estate unless I owned some of it. My salary here was so paltry it barely kept me in food.

Jen came hurrying in, her streaked and straightened hair gathered in a high ponytail. She wore a turquoise shell with a matching shrug, and a white skirt that stopped about half an inch above her knee. She had turquoise sling backs on her feet. The back of them had a little white bow right over the heel. She looked perfect. She always looked perfect. Perfect and cool.

"Hi Luis, Chere." She nodded at me. "I wondered where you'd gone to." The last was directed at me. Luis had his stubby fingers still clasped together, he watched us trying to figure out if we were friends or enemies. "Is there a problem Luis?"

"Chere's in here to discuss a raise."

"Raise? Chere are you due one?"

I nodded. Who cared if my double chins bobbed? I'd lost a chin so far with my weight reduction. I tried to read Jen's expression.

"In that case," Jen said, "a written evaluation would be in order. Chere how about you doing your own self assessment and submitting it to me."

"You know what I do," I shot back at her. "Why do I have to write anything down?"

One of her waxed eyebrows hit the ceiling. "If you want me to go to bat for you then you need to write down your accomplishments. It is money we're talking about."

"Uh, there's another thing," Luis interjected. "Chere feels that the column's name should be changed. She has a suggestion for what it should be called."

What a pot stirrer Luis was.

"Does she now?" I saw a glint in Jen's hazel eyes; a possible warning that she might hurt me. "We've taken up enough of your time," she said, giving me the look that said, "I better get up and follow her." So I did.

Outside she said, "What the hell was that all about?"

"I need money."

She waited until we were back in her office before responding. "Then you should have discussed it with me."

"I did."

"When?"

"Every chance I get." I grabbed a bunch of letters and began ripping the envelopes open.

Jen placed a hand on my shoulder. "Hon, you

know that I'll do what I can, but I really wish you'd spoken to me first."

"Trying to get some money out of that tightwad is impossible," I grumbled. "I was counting on him being afraid of Ian."

Jen narrowed her eyed. "And for that you made me look like a fool."

"I was sick of pleading with you. Nothing was happening."

"Okay, here's the deal. You start producing. You need to read at least twenty letters per day. If you can keep that up I'll see what I can do about bringing up your hourly rate."

"Can I have that in writing?" I threw back. Trust was not something I did easily.

"Fine."

Jen found a notepad and scribbled something which she then flipped at me. I caught it, scanned it and stuffed it into my hot pink purse that had purple flowers blooming off the front. I'd hold her feet to the fire if she didn't come through that's how desperate I was for money. I wanted to start living nicely like a real estate agent should, and in my own place.

"I don't suppose you got anything to eat?" I asked Jen when she was seated again and I'd determined she wasn't still mad. "I'm starving."

"No food, Chere, but there's plenty of work."

When she wasn't looking I stuck out my tongue. Childish, yes, but it relieved frustration.

Later that day, I took special care to dress, and all on account of me going to Quen's place. Being down a couple of dress sizes was reason to strut my stuff. I put on a pair of black capris and a long black T-shirt that covered my butt. Then I jazzed up the outfit with silver earrings and plunked a silver cuff on my wrist and then I put on my silver sandals with the little bitty heels.

I threw in a few curls with the hot iron and finger combed the new do. Short was growing on me. I hadn't worn my hair this short in years. So maybe Jen was right. I did have cheekbones and eyes. Eyes that I needed to play up. I got out the pencil and outlined the corners. Now I reminded myself of Diana Ross, thank God I had gotten rid of the weave.

I spritzed on some perfume—Jen's of course, and got into the elevator. Quen lived in the apartment across from Jen's other apartment that had been renovated. I'd called earlier about the grocery list but he'd said, "My treat this time. The next is on you."

But I didn't want to arrive empty handed and I couldn't think of a thing to bring? Colt wouldn't cut it. I needed something fancier. I wasn't a wine drinker and I didn't know the difference between vintage and shandy but I wanted to make a good impression so I settled on fruit. Stopping to buy it would have me running ten minutes later than planned but at least I wouldn't show up with my two empty hands.

I was standing, balancing the container of fruit in one hand and scanning the list of names on the directory. Finally I found Quen's name and I sucked in a breath and pressed hard on the buzzer.

"Chere is that you?"

"Yeah, yes it's me."

Gotta work on that elocution. Gotta keep remembering that.

The front door buzzed open and I entered. Two security guards manned a circular desk, although they knew me they just nodded, but I could tell the wheels were rapidly turning in their heads. They must be trying to assess the situation.

Smiling and waving I headed for the elevator. By the time I found 4E, Quen's door was slightly ajar.

I stuck my head through the opening. "I'm here," I called. "Sorry I'm late."

"Come on in, sugar." Quen's voice came from some place I couldn't see.

I took a minute to straighten my clothes. I plastered a smile on my face and entered. Quen's head was in the oven and all I could see was a nice toned butt. Delicious. The smell coming from that oven made me want to push him aside and dive into whatever he was cooking.

He snapped closed the oven door and turned to me, at the same time wiping his hands on a towel.

"You look great, sugar. Did I tell you how much I like your hair?"

He had mentioned it several times, telling me I looked like a young version of Anita Baker. I held out my fruit. "I brought this."

Quen took the bowl from me and glanced at the contents.

"It wasn't necessary but still nice of you." He set the fruit on the counter and turned his attention to what was cooking on top of the stove.

"Something smells good," I said.

"We're having turkey, wild rice and greens."

"Rice?" I repeated, frowning. "Isn't rice fattening?"

"Not if eaten in moderation. The body needs some carbs to function." He bent over, giving me another mouthwatering view of his butt, and removed turkey breasts from the oven. Then he turned off the stove. "I'll get us drinks."

While Quen was making drinks I wandered around the apartment, purposely avoiding the bedrooms. His decor was like him, clean, practical and to the point, totally different from my taste. The living room held a leather sofa, a matching lounger and ottoman. A low coffee table had health and fitness magazines fanned out on it. A rubber plant in one corner needed watering.

There were no window treatments to block the view so when you looked out of the sliding glass doors all you saw was beautiful, blue ocean. The dining area overlooked the ocean as well. It held a round glass table and four matching high-backed chairs. My slides clip-clopped against polished wooden floors as I stared out at that wide wonderful ocean.

The scent of citrus had me thinking of oranges. Quen handed me a frosty party glass with a clear liquid in it; a slice of lemon floating on the top. He clinked our glasses together.

"Here's to you, beautiful, and our new venture."

Hoping for a nice alcoholic drink I took a long sip and almost spat it out. Water! I tried not to show my disappointment.

"Water's good for you. Combined with lemon it

can be both cool and cleansing. Citrus combined with certain foods breaks down fats."

I smiled loving this moment of intimacy. Those chocolate-brown eyes were looking directly at me and my teeth were chattering. Hell, my knees were knocking, too. I wanted to knock boots with this man.

Easy, girl. You need to figure out how to get the attention of a man like him.

I went into real estate agent mode.

"Do we have a date set for our radio interview?" I asked, mimicking Cummings.

"As a matter of fact we do. Let's talk about it over dinner. Until then let's take this out to the balcony."

Quen swept my glass out of my hand and led the way.

A cooling breeze helped me simmer down. I watched gigantic palm trees swaying in the distance and I inhaled a strong smell of salt. On the boardwalk, a few energetic types jogged and mothers pushed babies in strollers. On the beach lovers walked hand in hand, stopping every now and again to embrace and kiss. I envied them; must feel good to be loved. I'd never been romanced. The kinds of men that came onto me didn't believe in that stuff.

I watched the sun dip behind the horizon and darkness slowly descend.

"This time of day is my favorite," Quen whispered. "It's beautiful and peaceful and makes you believe that tomorrow miracles can happen."

I needed a miracle to get to him.

Quen stood very close to me. His masculinity was intimidating and made me not think clearly. Having him this near and smelling so good made me want to rip off my clothes and beg him to take me. But I couldn't. I didn't want to scare him off. We'd come a long way from personal trainer and trainee to business partners. He didn't need to know I wanted more. Had always wanted more.

"Tell me about you?" he asked, surprising me. "What are Chere's hopes and dreams?"

"Right now getting by."

"Oh, come on, there must be more, sugar. You're an assistant to the town's advice diva. You've gotten a real estate license. I heard you were taking continuing education classes. Something must drive you?"

You. You. You. I wanted to shout.

He was waiting for my answer. No one had ever asked about Chere, the person before. I'd always been the fat funny woman that no one ever took seriously. Now where to begin and what parts to skip? Quen had probably heard a lot about me. It was rumored I slept around, and yes I'd had my share of men but I didn't just hop into bed with Tom, Dickie or Manny.

Quen's fingers stroked my upper arm. "If it makes you uncomfortable, sugar, you don't have to tell me a thing."

"I don't know where to begin," I admitted.

"Suppose I ask questions and you answer what you want."

"Okay."

"Were you born in Flamingo Beach?" Quen asked.

"No. I'm from New York. The South Bronx."

He lifted his head to the side and eyed me. "Rough neighborhood, or at least it used to be. How did you survive?"

"Best education I got was on those street. Better than the college degree it almost killed me to get."

I had my bachelors in journalism and was damn proud of it.

Quen took a long sip of water. I followed suit. He was making me thirsty.

"So what was your reason for moving here?" he asked.

I debated then thought what the hell.

"I fell in love with a man and followed him South. The minute he got to Miami he dumped me. I heard about Flamingo Beach and heard the living was cheap so here I am."

A muscle quivered in Quen's jaw but then again maybe it was my imagination.

"That was pretty courageous of you. Most people would have gone home to family and gotten some kind of emotional support."

"I'm independent," I said thrusting out my chest. "My mom taught me to be. My father was never around. And I make friends easily, besides people care here. In New York you're just one of many people struggling to get by."

Quen digested my comment but didn't say anything for a while.

"How did you get the job with the *Flamingo Beach Chronicle?*" he finally asked.

I had nothing to be ashamed of.

"Through the owner, Ian Pendergrass. When his wife died, Ian hired me to take care of his house. We became friends, real good friends. He kept telling me that I was too smart to clean house, he talked me into going to school and he got me the job at the *Chronicle.*

"That was nice of him."

"I thought so."

I didn't tell him Ian like my uncle had expected payback.

Quen took my hand and studied my palm. Jen had talked me into a French manicure and I wasn't sure I liked it. I was used to nail art, the kind that came with jewels and flowers, but she told me to stay safe and save the fancy stuff for when I was going places. Sheesh!

"Long life line," Quen said. "Do you like what you're doing?"

I hesitated before blurting, "It's a job and boring as hell. I'm sick of reading all those letters with people complaining."

"A good reason to get your real estate and property management licenses. I love running the gym and being a personal trainer but I knew I needed something else. Time to eat."

I followed him inside and helped him serve the meal. We sat at the table facing each other. I chewed on that delicious turkey and screwed up my courage. Finally I said, "I want to be somebody."

"You are somebody."

I hung my head. No man had ever spoken to me with such sincerity before, like I mattered. I was starting to sweat. I wanted the attention off me.

"What about you?" I asked. "I don't know a thing about you except what you told me the other night. You came back to town with a woman you married."

Quen chewed for a while. At first I thought he didn't hear me.

Why pussyfoot around. "What really caused the divorce?" I asked.

"Would you like another piece of turkey?"

I would sell my own mother for another slice of that bird. I waited until it was dished onto my plate.

"Well?"

I still wanted to know what had gone wrong with Quen's marriage and I wanted to hear it from him.

The second piece of turkey was more delicious than the first, either that or I was hungry. Even the steamed rice was good and the greens were like I'd never tasted.

"You and Joya seemed so happy," I fished.

"We were."

Quen began spooning rice rapidly into his face.

"Happy people usually don't get divorced."

Quen set his knife and fork down. His expression wasn't what you would call warm and friendly.

"You want the truth, sugar?"

I nodded. I was practically sitting on the edge of my chair waiting to hear the dirt.

"Joya did not want to be married to a personal trainer. She wanted a guy who went to work in a suit and tie. Much as I hate to say this we were lucky she had a miscarriage, or we would have been two people stuck in a very unhappy marriage."

I'd expected some big revelation; something that might make even Jerry Springer sputter, not something as stupid as that. I thought maybe he'd tell me Joya didn't like sex, or that she was a lesbian, or a man hater.

"I wasn't good enough for her. She wanted me to be something I was not."

I scrunched up my nose, "And you broke up because she thought you weren't professional?"

"Something like that."

It didn't make sense to me, but what did I know. I'd never been married. And Quen looked like a mighty fine catch. He held good conversations and had a job. Two jobs: one as a personal trainer and the other as a nutritionist. How much more could you expect from a man? Plus he owned three condos, and from what the girls told me the equipment down south was in fine working order.

"Manny's going to bring you the leases to sign tomorrow," I said changing the subject. "He thinks he might have the other apartment rented as well. Fingers crossed."

"That'll ease some pressure."

I'd cleaned everything off my plate and was hoping for dessert, something more substantial than the fruit I'd brought.

Quen swept me up with him, and began dancing me around the room. His mood had changed and the old carefree Quen was back.

"Guess what, sugar?" he said, "A week from today you and I are scheduled on the Jenna and Tre show. Think you can handle that?"

With Quen's arms around me I could handle just about anything.

But I needed to keep them around me, and that meant coming up with a plan.

Chapter 9

The following evening I was on my way to the bowling alley to meet Sheena when my cell phone rang.

"This is Chere," I said in my best Realtor voice. I'd forgotten to check my caller ID.

"It's Quen. Is this a good time to talk, sugar?"

"Always a good time to talk to you, hon."

Yeah, yeah, I knew I was flirting. But hearing his voice made my heart pound so hard that I had a hard time keeping the car on the road. I kept a death grip on the wheel of the Honda making sure I didn't sideswipe someone.

"I could just kiss you," Quen said, "Manny brought me those two leases. I'm in the money."

My stomach began to flip-flop. Did he just say he wanted to kiss me?

"What are you doing tomorrow night?" Quen asked.

"Nothing." I had elocution class, but shoot I could miss that at least once. I already had the basics down pat. It was a question of learning to speak like you had marbles in your mouth. Like you were a white woman.

"Good. I know this is late notice but I have tickets for a jazz concert and I'd like us to go together. It's outdoors so don't dress up. I'll pick you up at seven."

And just like that I had a date with Quen, although I wasn't sure it was a date. I had the feeling it was more of a thank you for helping him rent those two places. Whatever, I was going to spend time with him and that's what mattered. I planned on looking damn good.

I had a big old fat smile on my face by the time I sauntered into that bowling alley. Sheena was at the bar dressed in one of her hoochie mamma getups and draped over two men. She managed to untangle herself and came gliding over to me. She held a Colt in one hand.

I grabbed the bottle from her and took a big gulp, rewarding myself.

"You're late. I've been here half an hour already," Sheena complained, grabbing the bottle back.

It had been a while since I'd had booze and just that slug went straight to my head.

"You didn't waste any time getting busy," I said eyeing the two skanky men.

Sheena popped her fingers and did a chicken neck. "Women need to keep their options open. Come meet Morris and Parnell."

I really didn't want to meet any of those men but I couldn't very well diss them so I went over with Sheena.

Morris was the taller of the two. He was brown skinned and his short hair looked processed. What was it with these men and their updated curly perms. Morris had this big old gold tooth sparkling in his mouth. Parnell was shorter, rounder and darker. He seemed the quieter of the two.

"So this here's your friend, huh?" Morris said eyeing me like I was his dinner. "Girl, you got a name?"

At first I wasn't going to answer him then I thought might as well have some fun. I took out a couple of business cards and passed them around. Parnell, from the way his eyes popped, seemed impressed. He probably thought he'd found himself a meal ticket.

"You're in the real estate business," he said, making it sound as if I was out of his league. I wasn't used to this. It was usually the other way around.

I smiled. No actually grinned.

Meanwhile Morris was wagging his head and looking me over like I was a great big pizza pie. "Cher-e, Cher-e be-be," he began to sing.

"The name's Chere as in Sonny," I snarled. I didn't think it was all that funny. And yes there was a time that I might have led the two losers on and gotten my ego boost, but now that seemed a total waste of time. I just wasn't interested.

"I thought we were supposed to be bowling," I complained to Sheena.

"In a little while."

I didn't like the way that sounded. I wanted to do what I had come there to do and then go home and start planning my outfit for tomorrow.

I walked up to the bar, and as much as it killed me, ordered a diet soda. When I turned around Parnell was right behind me.

"What is it you do?" I asked him since he seemed the nicer of the two men.

"Ever hear of Dyson Luxury Limousines?"

"No." Okay, so I outright lied. I wasn't about to tell this guy that slick Dickie Dyson was always angling to get into my pants.

"Best dang limousine service this town has," Parnell added.

Richard, slime bucket that he is, must have his men brainwashed.

"You're a driver?" I asked.

"Yes, ma'am, and if you're not busy one of these nights I'd like to take you for a spin."

That would happen when hell froze over. At that point I made up my mind if Sheena wasn't bowling that didn't mean I couldn't bowl. I excused myself and hurried off to get shoes and a ball, praying that Sheena didn't let the beer go to her head and invite the two fools to join us.

As it turned out, Sheena never did bowl so I attached myself to one of the leagues; a group of people that I knew. I ended up getting several strikes.

At an early age I learned never ever to rely on anyone for anything, much less entertainment. I'm good at being independent, and as long as I am able I want to be able to run my own life.

Next day, because I wanted the day to go quickly, I applied myself to reading letters. Jen kept glancing up inquiring about my health. I ignored her, figuring she was just busting on me. We were working out of the *Chronicle*'s office and at the end of the day I reminded her of what she'd promised.

"Didn't you say something about a raise if I read twenty letters a day?" I asked.

"Something like that." She had her eyes fixed on that damn monitor and a pen clenched between her teeth. "But you need to do so consistently. Keep up the pace and we'll talk."

I snorted loudly. That must have broken her concentration because she removed a bottle of coral nail polish from her desk drawer and touched up her fingernails.

"You going somewhere special?" I asked.

"Jazz concert. Tre's radio station was giving away tickets."

I smiled back at her totally happy. I was beginning to join the ranks of the somebodies. "So am I," I said.

Jen looked taken aback, even surprised. "How come you didn't mention it before?"

"How come you didn't tell me you were going?"

"Because we just made up our minds."

We being her and Tre.

Jen dipped the brush back into the bottle and tightened the cap. She looked at me with what I interpreted as admiration.

"You have a date?" she asked.

"Yes, ma'am."

I gave her a mysterious smile and went back to my letter reading.

Let her wonder who. The last person she probably expected me to be out with was Quen. Quen Abrahams didn't need to take out Chere Adams, not when he could have his choice of any number of women. But he'd asked me and I planned on taking full advantage of that invitation. I was bound and determined to get him to notice me as a woman.

When I got home the first thing I did was get on the scale. I'd lost another couple of pounds and I'd guessed it because walking was becoming easier. I wasn't hauling around as much weight and I wasn't huffing and puffing as much, either. I didn't feel the constant need for an inhaler.

I tried on a bunch of clothes but none of my casual clothes fit. They were all loose and hung on me. I looked like a bag lady.

Since it was getting late, I went into the bathroom to take a shower. I lathered on some of the fancy gel Jen had left and let the needles of water pound my throbbing body. By the time I'd stepped out of the stall my head was clear.

Jen was my role model and everyone said she

was classy and put together. I'd often wondered what it was about her clothing that stood out. Personally I thought she needed more color. Her fashion sense wasn't exactly what you call happening, but she did keep things simple while mixing them up. She'd wear a velvet camisole top with jeans and a T-shirt tucked into a chiffon skirt. Somehow it all came together.

I decided to take a major leaf out of her book and do my own mixing.

Then the thought popped into my head what about a sarong? I could make that fit. All it required was wrapping long pieces of cloth around my middle and putting a knot on the side. If I wanted bling all I had to do was add a sparkly brooch. Now all I had to worry about was a top.

On our shopping spree, I'd bought a sleeveless top of some kind of stretch material that held you in and was supposed to make you look slimmer. It was black. But that was okay because the sarong I had in mind had red hibiscuses so the black top would be a perfect match.

Quen would be here in twenty minutes. I needed to hurry. I found the oversized scarf and looped it around my belly. It didn't look too bad. I pinned it securely so as to not have an embarrassing moment then I pulled the top over my head. Okay, I wasn't Halle, but who was? I finger combed my new do, worked on my make up, playing up my eyes and cheeks and shoved my feet into black open-toed wedges. Then I sprayed on Jen's perfume.

Just in time, too, because right then the doorbell rang. I gave a quick glance in the mirror and decided I was as pretty as any fat girl could be. If Quen didn't like me, too bad for him. Chest thrust out and chin up, I went off to answer the door.

"Hey, sugar." Quen stood in the doorway taking up space. As always he looked good enough to chow down on. He was wearing one of his short sleeve polo shirts, this time in an attractive shade of melon. He was wearing black walking shorts, the kind that circled his hips. A striped designer cloth belt pulled the look together. And he smelled like oranges. I wanted to devour him.

Removing one hand from behind his back he thrust a single rose at me.

"Look at you. I'll be the envy of every man in Flamingo Park. Ready?"

Dutifully I made a little circle enjoying the wolf whistle he gave me.

I thanked him for the rose and decided to carry it with me. I wasn't a blusher but honey chile I was blushing. I could get used to flowers. I gathered my purse and followed Quen out.

In the parking lot he held the passenger door of his convertible Sebring open and I slid in. We were going to arrive at the park in style. And everyone would know that I was his date.

It took several circles before we found parking that's how crowded it was. It's a problem when you live in a small town. Whenever there's a function every Dick, Jane and Harry are out on the rolling lawn, the cheaper seats were packed with people drinking beer and passing around cups filled with God knows what.

Quen kept a hold on my hand as he led me toward the more expensive area, close to the stage, and with a canopy overhead. On the way, we passed families picnicking, couples smooching and people hanging out. Everyone seemed determined to make a good time of it and all sorts of colorful cocktails circulated. Those bright plastic cups held piña coladas and daiquiris. Some might even hold Colt. I smelled the sweet fruity scent of different wines. I couldn't help thinking that I'd be here on the lawn with thc peoples if I'd come on my own.

As we continued on our way people called out to us.

"Hey, Chere!"

"Hey, girl."

"That you, Quen?"

"Yes, it is. Enjoy the show."

With a nod here and a greeting there we finally found our fourth row seats with a clear view of the stage.

"Great seats," I said, smiling at Quen. "How did you manage them?"

"Contacts, love. Tre is a good friend. Want something to drink?"

"Yes, please. Diet soda."

It was killing me. I wanted a Colt.

Quen nodded agreeably and went off to fetch our drinks. It was getting easier to be more disciplined now that the weight was coming off. My cravings for certain things were becoming more manageable.

"Is that you, Chere?"

I looked over at the couple seated on the far side of me. As luck would have it, it was Camille Lewis and her husband, Winston. Winston looked like this was the last place he wanted to be. I felt sorry for him having to listen to that woman all day.

I managed to nod and smile.

"You with Quen?" Camille shouted over the

noise of people chattering and at the same time managed to get quite a few of their attention.

I managed to nod again. I was smiling so hard the sides of my face hurt.

"Did you hear Joya's back in town?" she shouted.

I knew she was scheduled to arrive any moment I just didn't know when.

"Camille!" Winston elbowed his wife but that did nothing to stop her.

"That woman wants him back or why else would she be here. She left her flight attendant job and a big city like L.A. to come back to a place she's always hated."

I nodded again because I just couldn't speak. A big old lump had settled in the back of my throat and my chest felt tight. I needed my inhaler. What if Camille was right? What if Joya had come back to town to get Quen?

I got the inhaler out of my purse and gave it a good old squeeze.

"Joya's staying with her grandmother until she finds an apartment, at least that's what I hear," Camille continued to shout.

Another couple arrived and there was a whispered exchange.

"Sorry," Winston said, prying his wife out of her

seat. With relief I watched the newly arrived couple slide into the two seats and the old windbag and her patient husband leave.

Talk about ruining your night. Camille just got on my last nerve. She was one mean-spirited West Indian woman.

Another ten minutes went by and during that time half of Flamingo Beach came over to visit. I'd never been so popular in my life. Most of the people who came by were looking for something to flap their gums about. They probably wanted to know how someone like me had managed to get someone like Quen to take me out. Let them wonder.

A few seconds before the concert began Quen returned with our sodas.

"Sorry, sugar," he said, handing me my drink. "I must have run into everyone I know in this town."

"On purpose," I muttered. "Nosy bastards."

Quen either didn't hear me or chose to ignore me. He placed an arm around the back of my chair and I almost melted. Being with him made me feel good. I didn't want to ruin the mood.

And because I wanted our night to be special I decided he did not need to hear from me that Joya was in town. Tomorrow he could find out from someone else. Tonight was going to be about us.

And I planned on doing my best to make him forget that his size two ex-wife existed.

I was about to pull out all the stops.

Chapter 10

"Are you enjoying yourself?" Quen asked, in a raspy whisper that almost had me climbing out of my sarong.

I nodded. How could I not be having a good time I was with him.

I couldn't even put my good mood down to having too many drinks, either. It had been a magical night so far. A half moon had appeared in the middle of the saxophonist solo. I saw it as a good omen. Quen's arm was now draped around my neck. I squeezed my eyes closed and laid my head on his shoulder and pretended we were in love.

The alcohol was doing its job. The audience was singing along to an old Nat King Cole tune that Natalie had made famous again. A guitarist appeared on stage who sounded like Earl Kluge and the audience went wild. People were waving their hands in the air in time to the music, and I was swept away, half over the moon. I'd never gotten this much attention my entire life, both from the people around me and the man I was with.

When the concert finally ended there was a standing ovation. We stayed in our seats, deciding to wait out the crowd. As people filed by I could feel their eyes on me assessing the situation. I knew that by tomorrow I'd be the talk of the town. I was pretty sure I already was.

"We're thinking about getting coffee, want to join us?" a male voice asked Quen.

Tre and Jen had shown up from somewhere. I held my breath waiting for Quen to answer. I wondered if he'd had enough and couldn't wait to unload me.

"As long as where we go serves tea I'm on," he said. "You okay with that, sugar?"

I nodded. Okay? I was more than okay. I was pinching myself. The only thing better would be having Quen to myself.

"The diner then," Tre said. "Whoever gets there first grabs a table."

As it turned out Tre and Jen got to Mario's before we did. Quen kept the top of the convertible down and everyone we passed waved at us and had something to say to us.

When we arrived close to midnight, Mario's was still doing a brisk business. The Italian who owned it seeing the potential for a crowd had decided to stay open longer than his usual eleven.

Quen kept a hold on my hand and led me around the crowded tables. I couldn't miss the loud whispers and sometimes mean speculation. I knew they wanted me to hear.

"What's Quen doing with Chere Adams?"

"Think she's losing weight because of him."

"You would think he could do better."

It was said to make me feel like crap. Well I wasn't going to let any of these people pull me down. I felt beautiful and I thought I looked good. So I held my head high and linked my fingers through Quen's, and when I caught somebody staring I waved at them.

Tre was standing trying to flag us down. He'd found a table at the back of the room.

"There they are." I pointed Tre and Jen out to Quen.

We made our way over and Quen held out my chair and then took the seat next to me. Packed as the place was, there wasn't much room for maneuvering and when his leg brushed mine I just about died. Dammit I was getting horny.

"I hear you two set a date," Quen said after our orders had been taken.

"Finally," Tre grumbled. "I've been trying to convince this woman to marry me before I get away."

Jen punched his arm playfully. "I think it's the other way around."

"What are the plans? Big wedding? Small gathering? Eloping," Quen asked.

Tre spread his arms wide. "I am leaving it up to the lady. Whatever Jen wants Jen gets." He gave her that totally whipped look; the one that said he must be getting plenty.

I wanted Quen to look at me the way Tre looked at Jen. I was envious. I'd never been married and at thirty-three I was starting to feel like that might never happen. I wanted children; little folks that I could put my stamp on. My childhood had been awful and I planned on being protective. I'd be especially careful of having my kids around male adults.

"Yes, tell us about the wedding," I said to Jen.

She got all dreamy eyed on me. "I want to get married outdoors, maybe under a gazebo. I was thinking about someplace near the water where I could have a tent. Of course, there has to be music and lots of dancing. I want the long, white gown, veil, bridesmaids, flower girls, ring bearer, the whole bit. But it's going to be a beach party, loose and lots of fun."

"What about the honeymoon?" I was still pissed from being cut out of the cruise I'd won for us. This was before Jen had hooked up with Tre. Unbeknownst to her, I'd thrown a bunch of her business cards in for a Sun Ship cruise WARP had been promoting. Jen had won and although she'd promised to take me on that cruise with her she had yet to deliver.

"We haven't given much thought to where we're going yet," Tre said smoothly.

I snorted. Quen looked at me curiously. Just then the waitress returned with our tea. Jen and Tre had ordered cappuccinos and a slice of key lime pie to share. I think that woman was bent and determined to torture me.

Quen took a sip from his cup and set it down. "Planning a wedding is always stressful," he said. "God, I remember when Joya and I got married.

Granny J almost drove us crazy. The guest list kept growing and growing, and the expenses kept mounting. Every relative wanted a say. We almost broke up."

I wished he hadn't brought up Joya, it made me feel guilty for not telling him that I'd heard she was in town.

"Do I know Joya?" Tre directed the question to all of us.

Quen shook his head. "By the time you came to town she'd already taken off."

He didn't sound bitter at all. I wondered what that was about and I began to feel just a little bit fearful. What if the two had patched things up and Camille was right, that's why she was back in town?

The conversation shifted. Quen scooted his chair up next to mine and wrapped both arms around my shoulders. "Did Chere tell you she got my two apartments rented?"

Jen actually looked impressed. "That's really cool. Maybe you can start working on getting me a renter. Are the tenants local and have good jobs?"

I wondered whether she was trying to get me out and whether this was supposed to be a hint.

"I wouldn't rent Quen's condos to anyone who couldn't pay," I said, knowing I sounded annoyed. "Two of the tenants are from out of town. It's those two brothers who bought Carlton's Liquors. They're hiring someone local to run the store. I think they plan on turning it into some fancy wine and cheese place. The other is rented to that woman who sells time-shares for the new Flamingo Beach Spa and Resort."

"So why isn't she living at the hotel?" Jen asked. "From everything I heard it's supposed to be really upscale."

I'd asked Emilie Woodward exactly that question after Manny had had me do the paperwork. What she'd said made sense.

"She wants work to be separate from home. If she lives on the premises she'll always be on call."

"Good point!" Tre added.

The conversation shifted again and this time Tre took the lead.

"You set for your radio interview next week? I've been plugging you two every chance I get."

"We are, aren't we, sugar?" Quen gave my shoulder a little squeeze. Every time he laid a hand on me I went on fire.

"You're on the radio too? I knew about Quen, but I didn't know you were joining him," Jen said, looking directly at me. "How come you're keeping things from me?"

It really had slipped my mind. I was trying not to think about it. It wasn't as if I was a celebrity. I was going on the air to talk about weight loss and leaving myself wide open for all kinds of nasty comments. I was doing this to help Quen build his business, and because I realized that he liked slimmer women. I wanted to be slim. I was sick to death of everyone thinking that he could do better than me.

I watched enviously as Tre and Jen fed each other the slice of key lime pie using the same fork. I was jealous because neither of them had a weight problem, and doubly so because I wanted the kind of easy, intimate relationship they had.

"How did you get into nutrition and fitness, anyway?" Tre asked Quen after he'd fed Jen the last of that pie.

"Short version or long version?"

"Whatever version you feel like, just so long as Mario doesn't evict us."

I looked around. The place was just as packed as when we'd first entered, maybe more so. No one showed any signs of leaving soon.

"I used to be very heavy."

"You were not?" I had a hard time believing that, just look at him now.

"Yes, I was. You didn't know me back then. I

come from an overweight family with a myriad of health problems."

"Like what?" I asked.

"Diabetes, heart problems, high blood pressure. I lost an overweight sister at a fairly young age. Trust me that wakes you up." The muscles at the sides of Quen's jaws spasmed.

I hadn't heard this story before.

"What happened? Can you talk about it?" Jen asked softly.

"Vaughn was only twenty-five when she died. Collapsed in a grocery store and that was that. She left behind two children in South Carolina. Both are being raised by my brother-in-law and his wife."

"How horrible." The words rushed straight out of my mouth. I couldn't stop them.

"Anyway, that was my wake-up call. I was the youngest and weighed probably more than she did. I was determined not to go like that. I began exercising and eating right and I vowed to help as many people as I could. Now staying fit is a lifetime commitment."

His story was a sad one. I blinked back the water gathering in the corner of my eyes. It made me wonder if that's why he wanted to help me and if his only interest was in saving me and helping a fat woman slim down.

"Okay, guys let's talk about something else, like how good the concert was. That lead singer was off the chain," Quen said, aiming to get the conversation back on a more uplifting track.

"She sure was," Tre agreed.

People started slowly trickling out and Mario's help began piling chairs onto tables, signaling for the rest of us to leave.

"Guess it's time to call it a day," Tre said, standing, stretching and placing a handful of bills on the table. "WARP is paying for this," he said holding out his hand to Jen.

Quen steadied my chair as I attempted to get up, and all four of us headed for the exit.

We almost made it when a voice called from behind us.

"Hey, Tre, Quen."

I turned to see Camille, Winston and another couple leaving with us. We all groaned and Jen and I exchanged eye rolls. Jen shook her head silently signaling I shouldn't go off on the woman.

Camille was now almost on top of us.

"So what's this?" she asked, "It seems every time

I turn around I run into you two, and you tell me nothing's going on."

No one answered. We just continued walking. But that wasn't enough, Camille tapped Quen on the shoulder.

"Yes, Camille?" Quen's voice sounded a little strained.

"Did you know Joya's back in town." Quen's expression slowly changed from slightly annoyed to wary. His jaw clenched and unclenched. "She's staying at Granny J's until she moves into her own place."

And just like that my evening got ruined.

"Is there a reason you feel you need to tell me this?' Quen asked the pot stirrer.

Camille eyed him boldly. "You used to be married to the woman so I thought you would care."

"Why would I care?" Quen asked, his voice dangerously low.

"Camille!" This time it was Winston trying to get his obnoxious wife back in control.

Behind us a little crowd began gathering. We were blocking the exit.

I turned around. "What you people looking at?"

"Nothing."

A few slunk off but most held their ground. Nosy

as most of these people were they were smart enough not to tick me off. I told everyone I could, any chance I got, that I worked for *Dear Jenna,* and although few people associated Jen St. George with *Dear Jenna,* no one wanted to be featured in a column where only losers sought advice.

Camille was not about to give up. She was practically in Quen's face. "Well, from what I hear, Joya came back to town to make up with you."

"You heard wrong," Quen said, placing an arm around my waist. "Baby, it's time you and I get out of here."

We pushed by the people bottlenecking the door with Tre and Jen trailing us.

Outside, I heaved in a big mouthful of fresh air. And although my chest was tight, I refused to pull out my inhaler.

I hadn't been the one to break the news to Quen after all. The blabbermouth had, leaving me feeling insecure.

Now I had more to worry about than being overweight.

Chapter 11

I'd just started getting comfortable with this real estate business and was thinking I might even be able to make some money at it. My first commission check had taken care of some pressing bills and today I had another closing. I'd finally sold a studio apartment that had been on the market for months.

The buyer had wanted a quick closing and somehow I'd managed to pull it off. I was going to take that commission and use it as a down payment on a new car. I'd had it with my 1998 Honda and I needed something presentable to drive people around.

I sat in the conference room we used for closings, waiting for everyone to show up. Quen had kinda disappeared. I hadn't heard from him since the night of the concert and he'd had a substitute work me out. After that run in with Camille he'd seemed preoccupied and this led me to believe that maybe there was something to what Camille said.

If it was over then it wouldn't matter whether his ex was back in town or not.

I'd gotten myself so worked up I came close to having an asthma attack. But I simply refused to pick up the phone and call Quen. We had no understanding. He was free as a bird.

My cell phone rang, either the buyer or seller must be running late or maybe it was a new client. I picked up without checking the number. When you're an agent you hope every call is the one you're waiting for.

"Tell me there's been a huge mistake," Quen said.

No hello, no how are you, nothing. No excuse for disappearing.

"Mistake? What are you talking about?"

"How could you?"

"How could I what?"

"You know damn well what I'm talking about."

I was beginning to think he'd lost it. This was not the Quen I knew.

The conference room door pushed open and a man I'd never met walked in holding a briefcase. He looked like a lawyer and acted like one, too.

"I have to go," I said. "If you have something to say to me come by the apartment in an hour or so."

"Wait."

I hung up on him. My business was equally as important as his, and I didn't like his tone. I had no idea what I'd done to tick him off and no time to think about it.

"Ms. Adams. I'm the Cherry's attorney," the man said, sticking out his hand and handing me his card. After that people started to arrive; the buyer, the seller, Manny, the financer, all of the people involved in making a closing a closing.

As distracted as I was, I managed to get through the process, and at the end I got my reward. Money. The minute the door closed behind the last person, and it was just me and Manny I grabbed my purse.

"Hey, wait up a minute. Where you running to? Let's go have a drink to celebrate?" Manny asked, clamping a hand on my arm.

I pulled away and was halfway out the door

tossing my answer over my shoulder. "Maybe next week. I have to get home."

Now why did I say that? He'd be hounding me like a dog in heat until I agreed.

I wasn't home an hour when there was a knock on my door. After checking the peephole just to be sure, I let Quen in. He stood in the vestibule, arms crossed over his wide chest, biceps bulging. There wasn't even the hint of a smile on his face. Man oh man he was pissed.

He said nothing. I said nothing. We stood waiting each other out. I still couldn't think of a thing I'd done to piss him off.

Then finally Quen said, "I thought I could trust you, Chere, and then you do this to me?"

"Did what to you?"

"You go behind my back and rent my apartment to Joya without consulting me."

"Come again?" He must be on drugs. He just wasn't making sense. I knew who'd rented those condos and Joya's name was not on the lease.

"Don't play me. I heard it from Granny J herself."

Now I was really getting ticked. I didn't understand what was going on and I didn't like being accused of something I didn't do.

"You signed the leasing agreements," I shot back

and then I started ticking off on my fingers. "Apartment number one rented to the New Yorkers, Peter and Dustin Millard, the men who bought Carlton's liquor shop. Apartment number two rented to Emilie Woodward, director of sales and leisure at the Flamingo Beach Resort and Spa. What am I missing?"

I could tell from the way Quen's shoulders drooped he was losing his steam. "So how could this happen?"

"How could what happen? Speak in plain English."

Uninvited Quen walked into the apartment and flopped down in her chair.

"I ran into Joya at the grocery store," he admitted. "Stupid me assumed she'd be staying with Granny J then she dropped the bomb. She's subletting an apartment."

I still wasn't getting it. "Why would you care?"

"Because it's my apartment she's subletting."

"Oh!" I began to wheeze and was in serious need of my inhaler.

"You okay?" Quen asked

"Just give me a minute to digest this." I knew I sounded like a skipping CD. "Joya is subletting one of the apartments you gave me to rent?"

"Yes, when she first told me she'd be living at 411 Flamingo Place and gave me the apartment number, I thought someone must have it in for me. Mind you I don't think she knew it was mine or that I even lived in the complex."

Quen looked at me as if he expected an explanation. I had to think about it. How could Joya have gotten over o both of us.

"Sublet," I repeated focusing on that word. "If Joya sublet the condo it means she rented it from one of the people it was leased to. Either Joya found the Millards or they found her." I held up a finger. "Wait! Granny J's quilt shop is next door to Carlton's store. Peter and Dustin bought him out so maybe they worked something out with your ex."

There was a huge silence as Quen took it all in.

"Shit!" I'd never heard him curse. "Looks like I owe you an apology, sugar." He gave me one of his gooey-eyed looks. I didn't melt this time.

If he wanted me to forgive him he needed to come with something stronger. At the very least I deserved a kiss combined with some major groveling. Deep down I was still hurt.

"So," I said. "Now that you know what you know, what are you going to do about Joya subletting your place?"

Quen shrugged. “There isn’t much I can do? Joya’s probably already given them money and signed the lease.”

I placed my hands on my hips and gave him a chicken neck. I was supposed to be working on being classier but this called for street. “I’m going to find my copy of the lease, sugar, and then I’m goin’ read the fine print. Since you’re the landlord maybe you should do the same. If you’re real lucky there might be a clause that says no subletting.”

“Shouldn’t you have pointed that out to me?”

“It was your lease.”

Shift the blame.

“Shoot I need a reason to stop this from happening,” Quen said.

“You’re the landlord. I’m just the Realtor,” I added, getting smart.

What had me ticked off was it didn’t sound like he wanted to deal with this and it made me wonder if Quen still had feelings for his ex. I heard Camille Lewis’s voice in my head. *Joya came back to town to make up with you.*

“I suppose I could discuss the situation with the Millard brothers,” Quen said out loud.

“Whatever you want to do.”

Quen got out of that chair. He approached and

took me by the shoulders. "I'm really sorry, sugar. I was shocked when I heard and I overreacted. I should have known you would never do something like this to me. Am I forgiven?"

He hugged me to him and I stood on my tiptoes, my arms wrapped around his neck. I felt the slightest whisper of a kiss against my temple, and my stomach and my lower parts got all fluttery. I pressed against Quen and swore I felt a growing erection. He wasn't treating me like his little sister anymore. He was reacting to me like a man reacts to a grown woman.

Only a fool wouldn't take advantage of this. I'd been called a lot of things all my life, but never a fool. So I used what I had. Those triple Ds can make a grown man act stupid. I made them work for me now. I pressed my nipples against Quen's chest and made purring little noises like a contented pussy cat.

That erection was getting bigger by the minute and those kisses against my neck and temple were getting more wet. He was pressing himself up against me, too. Rubbing up against my pubis. I was in heaven. When Quen dipped his head and gave mc a kiss, our first real kiss with tongue and everything, my head spun.

I was moist all over and my limbs were like

rubber. There wasn't a doubt in my head what I wanted to happen next. Neither of us were kids, and we'd known each other a real long time. I was in love with the man; truly, madly, hopelessly in love. And I wanted him to be truly, madly, hopelessly in love with me back. So I used what I had. It was the only way that I knew how to get my point across

Plus I needed an edge over Joya.

It may not make much sense to you, but it made a heck of a lot of sense to me. I needed to get Quen's attention through whatever means I could. I had a woman in town that he'd loved enough to marry and from my recollections she was a pretty hot babe. Hot enough to attract the attention of some pretty fine men. Now that she'd become a flight attendant she probably looked even better. She was flying the world, going to places that I'd only dreamed of or seen in movies, meeting all kinds of people, and eating fancy foods. Joya had created for herself a totally different life than me.

When Quen kissed me again I lost all of my self control. My hands clawed his chest, searching and finding the buttons of his shirt. I slid a couple of fingers through an opening, and felt the heat coming off his skin. I stroked his warm flesh and made a few circles in the patches of hair.

"Oh, sugar." Quen's soulful sigh did it. I wanted to melt into him.

He placed an arm around my waist and half carried me and half dragged me up against the wall. He was breathing heavy. I was breathing louder; all on account of my asthma, of course.

I was the one who reached for his belt buckle. He saw that as permission to go for my breasts. He pushed my top up and over my head and buried his face in my cleavage. He licked, lapped, nuzzled and generally drove me crazy with want. I popped the clasp of my bra and served him my boobs. I wanted him to eat me all over. I finished unbuckling his belt and with one hand felt around.

My nipples weren't the only things that were rock hard and swollen. Quen Abrahams wanted me as much as I wanted him and unlike Manny he had length, volume and a hefty circumference. He was everything an active woman wanted in a partner.

I was still in my pants when Quen positioned himself between my legs and began sliding in and out. The friction alone created a fire that burned. I kept crying out, clawing him and calling, "Make me happy, let's do it already."

I wanted him inside of me and I didn't want to wait for a nice comfortable bed. Not when we were on fire and I was on the verge of living a dream. If we stopped I was afraid I might wake up.

"We should take this into the bedroom, sugar," Quen panted. He was echoing my thoughts but not necessarily my wishes.

We were still in the living room, hugging that wall and looking out onto the ocean. We could see out no one could see in and see us. Something about doing it here, half clothed with my boobs smashed against Quen's face and him sucking my nipples turned me on. Quen's pants rode his knees and Ole Johnson was primed and ready for entry. I was beyond warm. Girlfriend was hot. Sizzling.

"Sugar? We need to go into the bedroom now."

"Let's just enjoy each other and see where we end up," I said boldly.

Like I didn't know how this was going to end.

"Get out of your slacks." Quen sounded hoarse, as if he'd run several laps.

I experienced two seconds of uncertainty. My thighs, not my best assets, were like ham hocks. Oh, what the hell! We were too far gone to be thinking what looked good and what did not. It was about sensations, feelings, scratching an itch I'd had for years. It was about loving a man who'd never expressed interest in me as a woman until now.

I ripped off those capris and probably ripped them in the process. I scrambled out of my thong panties and made a silent note to get myself over to Victoria's Secret and buy me some more. My mother who was no lightweight, God bless her departed soul, used to say, "Fat don't have to mean sloppy. You can still be stylin, girl."

I'd taken her literally, and that explained all the wild clothes.

Quen was still obsessing over my boobs and I was obsessing over his member. As good as that thing looked I just knew he knew how to use it. He slid a hand between my legs and I damned near hit the ceiling. We were both breathing hard and rubbing up against each other.

Then he nudged my legs apart and began teasing, just giving me a little taste of what he could do when he really got going. I was loving all that brown skin and relishing the scent of sex mixed up with oranges.

This was my chance, maybe my one chance to make him remember me. Better pull out every last stop now before we really got going. I slid down the wall and got on my knees. Quen stood over me with his goods exposed. I took him into my mouth and began exploring. I teased him just like he'd teased me.

"Baby, enough," he said.

Quen eased me to the floor and climbed on top of me. My hands squeezed his buns and he pressed into me. He slid inside of me all warm, wet and wonderful. I was feeling him big time and when I tightened my muscles I knew he was feeling me.

"Sugar!" Quen gasped over and over again, pumping in and out of me. "You make a man want to climb Mount Everest over and over again."

I was beyond thinking. Every nerve came alive and my muscles were twitching. I was wired and ready. I arched my back and we found our own rhythm when Quen stroked my nipples I came close to spilling.

"Oh, lordie, lordie, lordie, Mommy's about to come," I shouted.

"Pappy's right with you baby."

And with that, Quen slammed into me, and all hell broke loose. We heaved, shuddered and cried out words no God-fearing person should know. He took me with him to a place where I'd never been before and this time it didn't require faking.

Quen Abrahams was turning out to be everything I'd hoped he would be and more. He'd surpassed my requirements in every single department.

Now I was more determined than ever not to let his ex get her mitts into him. I'd see to it that she packed up quickly and went back to L.A. and her fancy job.

Quen Abrahams was going to be mine. And I planned on being a heck of a lot more than a booty call.

Chapter 12

"I'll take a half a pound of that shrimp and one of those pieces of salmon. A small piece," I said to the grocer at the Flamingo Beach Mart.

Mac weighed the items, wrapped them in brown paper and handed them to me.

"Thanks," I said and shoved them into my cart.

Quen had done his disappearing act again. I hadn't heard from him since that night we knocked boots and I was starting to feel really insecure. I thought maybe he was avoiding me. He'd even had that substitute work me out again.

I was trying to figure out what was really going on here. Maybe he was feeling bad that he'd allowed things to go so far. I don't know what goes on in these men's minds. All I know is that after the kind of loving he and I had, he should have been more attentive.

It wasn't like I was expecting roses or anything, though that would be nice. But a phone call, how much did that really cost. We had a radio interview coming up in a few days I would think he would want to practice.

My imagination was going wild and I blamed it all on Joya. I'd heard about situations where a man has such good sex with another person he feels the need to have relations with the previous partner just to keep the memories real and in perspective. It happens I suppose.

"See you in a few days," Mac, who I'd known for a long time, shouted at my back.

"Bye, Mac."

During the last four days since Quen and I had gone at it, I'd cleaned out Jen's refrigerator and kitchen cupboards, getting rid of anything that looked like it might be fattening. I'd read the labels and counted the calories. Now I had real incentive to lose weight. Size two was not going to get the better of me. No way. No how.

I wheeled my cart past the diet food aisle and made a face. I couldn't quite go there yet. Cottage cheese, yuck! U-turning, I headed for the produce section. Salads could be mixed with chicken, turkey or fish.

As I bent over and began squeezing the tomatoes who comes rolling a cart up the aisle, Joya Hamill, that's who. I doubted that she would even acknowledge me, we did not move in the same circles. Never had. But she slowed down, looked me full in the face and said, "Hello, Chere."

I didn't think she even knew my name.

"Joya, right?" I pretended surprise. "You've been gone a real long time."

"Have I? Seems just like yesterday."

She gave me a false smile and I made myself smile back at her. She wanted something so I decided to play wait and see.

"How ya doing?" I asked.

"Fine."

I tossed a couple of tomatoes in a plastic bag, set them in my cart and waited. She said nothing.

"How long will you be in town?" I asked.

She shrugged and let out a sigh. "That's still to be determined. It depends on a lot of things."

To my disgust, Joya looked younger and fresher than ever. She was wearing low-riser short shorts and a red camisole top that left her flat stomach bare. She had her hair bunched up in a ponytail and tied back by one of those scrunchie things, and she wore a baseball cap the same color as her top on her head. On her feet she wore four-inch platform wedges which brought her eye level.

"Like?" I probed.

"Like my life straightening out. I'm sort of in no-man's land right now living out of a suitcase until I can get into my apartment."

"I thought you were staying at your grandmother's," I said, and waited.

"Only for a short time."

Joya showed no signs of moving on. She must want something. Several of the shoppers thought so, too, because I'd never seen more produce being squeezed in my life. The shopping carts had practically bottlenecked.

"I'm sorry we'd didn't run into each other before," I said in my brightest Realtor voice while fumbling through my purse. I found my Realtor card and flipped it at her.

Joya scrutinized it carefully then smiled at me.

"You're in real estate? The last I heard you were working for the *Chronicle* and before that cleaning houses for the owner."

A direct hit.

My smile was equally as bright.

"I still work for the *Chronicle* and am up for promotion," I answered. "Real estate is a sideline. If you'd come to me I could have helped you find an apartment." I made sure to sound proper just like she did.

Joya flipped her ponytail and placed both arms on the shopping cart, leaning in, speaking in a low voice as if we were the best of friends.

"Thank you, but I got lucky," she confided. "The New Yorkers who bought the shop next to my grandmother's needed some one to manage the business temporarily. They rented an apartment here and I'm subletting from them at an incredibly low price."

Kind of like my agreement with Jen. I didn't like this. Didn't like it one bit. If Joya was only in town for a short time why would she need a job. And why would she need an apartment?

"Weren't you waitressing or something in Los Angeles?" I asked, being bitchy.

Her ponytail swished again. "I'm a flight attendant but I needed a break so I took a leave of absence."

It must be nice to be able to walk away from a job, money and benefits. Maybe Quen was still paying her alimony. I was tempted to ask but decided not to go there.

"Well it's nice seeing you," I said, and started up the aisle.

"You, too," Joya called after me. "Maybe you and I can have a drink sometime."

Yeah, right! Why would she suddenly want to have a drink with me? We'd never been friends.

"Sure. You have my number," I called over my shoulder.

"Wait up. Let me give you mine." Joya sprinted up the aisle to catch up with me.

She dug into her designer purse and found a pen and scribbled her number on the back of her grocery list. Then she tore off a piece of the paper and handed it to me.

Pretending to be pleased, I thanked her.

"What the hell you looking at?" I hissed, rolling my cart right past the Nosey Parkers and heading for the diet food. I'd eat it all even if I choked. After seeing those spindly legs of Joya's I needed to drop several dress sizes and fast so that I could squeeze into my shorts. I was bound and determined to get down to a size fourteen dress and I needed to get there soon.

Later that day, after I'd called up everyone in

town to get the full scoop on Joya Hamill, I also decided to get my lard butt back to elocution class. Earlier, Ms. Thang had sounded like she had marbles in her mouth. I'd always thought of her as an uptown girl and high maintenance. The buzz was that she'd pushed Quen constantly, urging him to make it, to be somebody other than a personal trainer. To hear some speak she'd pushed him right out of her life. What it boiled down to was that it was all about her and the material things that made her a happy camper.

Whatever. Quen married her so there had to have been something that appealed to him. More reason than ever for me to get myself to elocution class tonight. And if it meant conjugating every last verb then so be it.

I had that interview coming up as well and I didn't want to sound like some fat, dumb woman Quen had picked up off the street. If I was going to be his spokesperson I needed to look and act the part. And as much as I hated to ask for help I needed to call on another black female with class and style. I picked up my cell phone and called Jen.

"Yes, Chere?" she said sounding a bit suspicious of me. She was probably still ticked about me going over her head and asking Luis for a promotion. I explained what I needed then held my breath.

"You want me to help turn you into something you're not?" she asked in a tone I didn't know how to interpret.

I chose to think she wasn't putting me down.

"I want you to help me become a lady," I repeated. "Please."

"First you need to think of yourself as a lady. Aren't you taking diction classes or something like that?" Jen asked.

"I am but it's not enough. I need to learn to walk the walk and talk the talk."

There was a huge pause on her end. "Why now, Chere? What brought this about?"

She wasn't stupid and I didn't feel like lying.

"I ran into Joya in the grocery store today."

"Yes, so? You knew she was in town."

"She's skinny and she talks just like you," I wailed. "I need to learn how not to sound like something other than street. I need to get this weight off. I want to wear cute little outfits with my belly hanging out. I want to be the girl that classy men take out. Well no, not just any classy man, I want Quen to look at me and want me."

"He seems to like you fine just the way you are.

I saw the way he looked at you at Mario's," Jen said dryly.

My heart beat a rat-a-tat-tat. "And how's that?" I needed affirmation.

"Like you were his sugar and he couldn't wait to lap you up."

"He did lap me up." I caught myself. I'd said too much. I swore loudly.

I heard laughter on the other end. But Jen seemed quite serious when she spoke. "Are you trying to better yourself for you or Quen?"

"For both of us."

I meant every word. My reinvention had been a long time coming. I was willing to change for Quen because I wanted him. But my life hadn't been that wonderful hauling around my weight. I was always tired, breathing heavy and needing an inhaler. My clothing had a tendency to bunch up and grab me in the crotch. Men that I wanted didn't seem to want me. And that left me being hounded by winners like Richard Dyson and Manny Varela, who would go with about anything that was female.

My makeover was long overdue.

Jen broke into my thoughts. "You're expecting a crash course, to be whipped into shape for your radio interview? I can't work miracles, hon. It's only a few days away."

"I was hoping you could. Just help me get through it without embarrassing myself."

"That I might be able to do, but anything else is going to take time, just like losing weight the healthy way takes time."

Time was not something I had on my side, especially with Joya back in town and looking as good as she did.

Desperate times called for desperate measures. I was starting a crash diet beginning now. And I was going to pay attention to every last word Mr. Cummings had to say tonight.

"Bravo, Ms. Adams, bravo. You're finally getting it." Mr. Cummings said, applauding me.

The homeboys in the back of the class rolled their eyes and broke into applause.

The obnoxious man had dragged me up in front of the class and had me translate a paragraph from Ebonics into his queen's English. I'd done it to his liking I guess.

"You go, girl," one of the homies shouted.

I took a little bow and skipped back to my seat. For the rest of the evening I paid close attention to everything Cummings said and everything he wrote on that blackboard. And at the end of the class as people were slinking out, he curved a finger at me.

"Ms. Adams may I see you for a moment?"

What, now?

I approached his desk hesitantly. Cummings looked at me over those red glasses of his. He actually smiled, a first for him. I'd always thought if that happened his face would crack.

"You are coming along, Ms. Adams. You have made amazing improvement. Don't be surprised if the class votes you valedictorian. You would do well to prepare a speech, just in case."

I hadn't expected him to praise me but it felt good to be singled out in a good way. I got all choked up and before I totally lost it, raced away.

Much as I hated the thought of it, I needed to talk to Dickie Dyson about a car and I needed to get over to his place before the close of business. My old Honda had taken to hiccupping and burping and I was afraid that one day it would leave me stranded. Even if I could afford to put money down on a new one, which I couldn't, my credit was so screwed up no one would fund me. And I couldn't afford the monthly car payment for a new one.

Manny told me that Richard sometimes sold his used sedan's to private citizens instead of trading them in. I'd found out through one of his people that he had a couple of cars that might serve my purpose. So I was bent and determined to renew our acquaintance.

As luck would have it, when I swung through Richard's double doors with the bright red lettering on the outside, he was inside his fish tank of an office. Before I could announce myself to the receptionist he came bolting onto the floor.

"Hey, fine thang." He moved in as if to kiss me and I moved safely out of range. Richard looked me up and down and made a face. "You're too skinny. You're losing weight and in all my favorite places."

"I thought that would be a good thing," I shot back watching his eyes linger on my chest and move down.

"A good thing for who? A man needs something to hold on to."

Mind you he's saying this loud enough for everyone to hear, making it clear that ours was an intimate relationship. The key word is was.

"Can I talk to you privately?" I asked, inching my way toward his glass cubicle.

"Sure thing. I knew you'd eventually come around."

The skinny bugger's moustache was practically jumping up and down as he hotfooted back to his office.

Richard waved me into a red velour swivel chair and took a seat in a leather high back one.

"Richard Junior misses you," he said boldly.

"I didn't think he ever got homesick."

I kept it light I needed to play this carefully. I wanted something. Richard wanted something.

"Let me show you just how much."

Richard stood up from behind his desk and surely enough he had a huge bulge in the front of his pants. I thought I would die.

"We need to talk business," I quickly said before things got out of hand.

Richard got serious. "What kind of business? You better not be telling me the rabbit died cause its been months since you let me touch you."

"Almost a year." What I wanted to add but didn't, is that I didn't feel as if I was missing a thing.

"Much too long and I'm not real happy about it."

"I want to buy one of your used limos," I said, to get him off the subject. "And you'll need to finance me."

"You're here because you want to buy one of my vehicles?"

"Uh-huh."

"Which one you want?"

He had to be pulling my leg, but he was actually sounding agreeable, so to test him I pointed out the window at the longest limousine in the parking lot.

"What about that one?"

"It's yours." Richard named a figure that damn near choked me. He must have seen my face. "There's a van with low mileage that I've been thinking of getting rid of. I use it for pickups and drop-offs at the airport and not much else. Most who lease a limo are looking to go places in style. Vans are for families, church groups and athletic teams. This van isn't bringing in the income I hoped."

I brightened. "So you'll sell it to me."

"Umm, hmm. But there are conditions."

I hadn't thought of a van but it just might work. It was practical and newer than the Honda. Plus it would be good for running clients around in.

"How much do you want for it?" I asked, ignoring his "conditions."

Richard thought for a moment. "I'd make it affordable and we'd work something out."

"How soon could I have it?"

"As soon as you want."

"I could leave with it tonight?"

"Yes, you could."

This was much too easy. And Richard still hadn't discussed his conditions with me.

"And how would the payments work. Do you need a deposit?" I asked.

He thought again. "Nah, I don't need a deposit from you. You're a friend. The van's all paid for so you'd pay me directly."

I don't know what possessed me but I kissed Richard on the cheek. And of course he grabbed me up and kissed me on the mouth, right in that fishbowl of an office where everyone could see.

Wouldn't you know it, Quen chose that moment to walk in. He saw what was happening and walked out again.

I pushed out of Richard's arms, and, not caring how it looked, went running after him.

"Quen!" I shouted. "Quen!"

But he didn't break stride. So I kicked off my shoes and started to sprint.

"Quen!"

Chapter 13

I caught up with Quen as he was getting into his car. I leaned my big fat butt against the front of that car and dared him to drive away.

I knew he had heard me running after him. My heels had been thudding loudly against the pavement and my breath was coming in great big pants.

He started up the engine. There was no way he would move off.

I didn't move and finally he turned the car off and got out.

We faced each other.

"You could do a heck of a lot better than Richard Dyson," he said.

"I'm not doing Richard. I went in to buy a car. Where have you been, anyway?"

I didn't owe Quen an explanation but at the same time I didn't want him thinking I was a "ho."

I know I sounded like I owed him, but, in fact, he was the one who owed me an explanation for dropping off the face of the earth. We'd made love like it was going out of style and then he'd up and disappeared

Quen's expression didn't encourage questions. His face looked like he'd eaten something sour.

"I needed a few days to sort some things out. I needed space."

"Umm, hmm. So when do we start back exercising again?" I needed something concrete, a reason to hope.

"I was thinking that you might be better off with another trainer."

"What!" I moved in closer until the smell of oranges filled my nose. "How am I going to be your spokesperson if you and I aren't working out together and you're not watching what I eat?"

He looked at me for a long time and then he said,

"I've been thinking about that. Maybe we should ditch that plan."

I was so frustrated by then and damn close to crying, I punched Quen in the arm.

"I know why you're doing this," I said. "And I'm not going to let you."

His fingers clamped down on my wrist and he pulled me close to him and looked me in the eye. "It's wrong what I did. I'm your trainer and I shouldn't be having a personal involvement with you. It'll just confuse things."

"Says who?" I shouted back. "Don't I have a say?" Call me demanding but I wasn't just going to step aside and let him walk away.

"Chere, you have plenty of men interested in you. You're looking to trim down and improve your health and right now you don't need any involvements."

It sounded like B.S. to me, as if he had rehearsed this speech and was hell-bent on delivering it.

I stabbed one of those big biceps with my fingernail. "You mean *you* don't need any complications. You're just bent out of shape because Joya's back in town and you're having a hard time dealing with that. You and I have been friends for too long for you treat me like this."

Quen gave me one of those sideways looks. I just knew Richard and the employees in his office had their noses pressed against the glass panes as they stared out onto the lit parking lot, and watched the drama. I didn't care.

We stared each other down until Quen looked away. A slow grin spread across his face. "You are one feisty woman. Yeah, I'm dealing with stuff, and yeah it's not easy having your ex-wife pop up again and move into a place that you own."

"I understand," I said bobbing my head. "It's a lot to handle. Just as long as you and I are okay, that's all I care."

My palms were still clammy but I needed reassurance. I didn't want to scare Quen off by telling him I loved him.

"Ah, sugar," he said on a deep sigh. "You are by far the best lover I've ever had. We connected. You were all the things you read about. Open, loving, adventurous, wild and crazy. That's why I'm thinking this isn't good. We need to put distance between us. You need a trainer who's fully engaged in helping you to get weight off."

"Quen," I pleaded. "We're doing a radio interview in a few days. The entire town is going to tune in.

There's been advertisements on the radio. You and me are a package. This is business not personal."

He started to laugh. "You don't give up do you?"

"No. All I want is to go back to the way we were. It was comfortable. You're the bestest friend a woman could ever have. If we happen to end up in bed again, then we'll write it off to shit happening," I added slyly. "Now excuse me, I gotta go see a man about a car."

Quen kissed me on the cheek. "You're something else, sugar," he said. "See you tomorrow at six. Don't be late."

"I won't."

I blew him a kiss and headed back for Dickie's.

My mother used to say I could sell ice cubes to Eskimos. I'd just sold an entire ice sculpture.

I drove off from Dyson's Luxury Limousines with that Mazda minivan. Richard said I could give him the down payment later and he would go ahead and arrange the transfer of ownership. I knew he wanted me to owe him, but I needed a vehicle and so I decided to deal with the issue when it reared its ugly head.

My radio interview was in two days, and I was starting to get nervous. What if I said something stupid? I didn't want to embarrass Quen. The idea was to talk up the weight loss program and the nutrition business. If I did good I was already fantasizing how our evening would end.

For the next two days I agonized and spent hours practicing my diction and rehearsing with Jen. By the time the interview rolled around I felt fairly confident.

Quen and I had decided to arrive separately. I showed up driving the green minivan, parking it right next to Quen's Sebring. I'd seen him that morning for a forty minute workout session and things between us were back to normal. Almost.

Instead of taking the elevator, I walked up the stairs. Quen was seated in the waiting room when I walked in and he got up and came to greet me.

"Nervous?" he asked, holding my hand.

"A little. The biggest problem will be for me to remember the grammar stuff. I don't want to embarrass myself or you, and I sure as hell don't want to sound ghetto."

"You'd never embarrass me. Just be yourself." He chucked me under my chin. He was back to treating me like a little girl.

He got us both a cup of water from the cooler and we sat shooting the breeze. A young boy, who looked like he'd barely hit puberty, came to get us. He introduced himself as the assistant producer.

Tre waited inside a tiny box of a room. Quen whispered to me this was the broadcast booth.

"Hey," Tre said, waving us into two seats. "We're on in five." He had earphones looped around his neck like a dog collar.

We had a quick briefing as to the kinds of questions he would ask. So far it didn't seem like it would be too difficult.

"Once we open the phones and the listening audience call in," Tre said, "expect anything. You can choose to answer questions or not."

"You're on the air in ten," the production assistant mumbled, sticking his head in the booth.

I sucked in a deep breath. My palms were clammy and I felt the beads of sweat on my upper lip.

"You'll be fine, sugar." Quen gave my hand a little squeeze. "Now breathe."

"Five, four, three, two, one," the assistant called.

Quen gave us the thumbs up and started in.

"Yo Flamingo Beach, D'Dawg here. Tonight joining me are two of the Beach's most popular black folks. Give a shout out to Quentin Abrahams, most of you know him as Quen, and Chere Adams, who has two jobs one as Realtor and the other at the *Chronicle.* How you folks doing tonight?"

"We're doing just fine," Quen said speaking into the microphone and nudging me with his elbow.

"Doing great," I said, my voice sounding all quivery.

"Quen, as most of you know is a personal trainer and a nutritionist. He's here to talk to you about getting rid of those love handles. So how do we get a body like Will Smith or Halle Berry?" Tre asked.

"Actually I'm not here to tell anyone they should look like a movie star," Quen said, which made me want to kiss him. "People who want to lose weight need to do so for themselves. They need to set goals and have reasonable expectations. Everyone's body type is different. Some of us carry extra pounds better than others. Instead of trying to look like something you're not, work with what you have."

"Okay, so pretend I'm a thirtysomething woman and I'm lugging around a couple of extra pounds. What would you tell me?"

"I'd tell you that you should be working out with a personal trainer. If you can't afford it then walk every chance you get. And make sure your diet is balanced."

"And is this what you're doing with Chere, supervising her calories?" Tre asked. Boy was he good at shooting questions at us.

"Yes, he does," I said quickly. "I've already lost a total of twenty-six pounds. I've surpassed a personal goal. The man's a genius." I was gushing.

"Well, you go girl!" Tre said focusing his attention on me. "What made you go to Quen for help?"

"Any man who looks this good had to be doing something right."

Quen cleared his throat. "You're making me blush, sugar."

He'd said *sugar* loud and clear on the air for anyone to hear. I thought I might faint.

"Did I hear something about him cooking you meals?" Tre asked.

"Yes, Quen has these recipes and he cooks me meals that are healthy."

We hadn't quite started cooking yet, but the only way Tre would have known about the meals was if Quen had told him, so I felt safe telling a little white lie.

"Sounds cozy to me," Tre said to Quen, giving a raspy chuckle. "And you're telling me that anyone who wants to lose weight can sign on with Quen and he'll be their personal chef."

"I'll happily work up a menu," Quen said amiably. "I do offer options. The client can either purchase foods already prepared or they can get recipes. If they want both I will be glad to comply."

"I am guessing none of this comes cheap. So how does someone find out about pricing?"

"I have a Web site," Quen said and quickly gave the URL.

"And I'm proof that his weight loss program works, and I have the before and after pictures to prove it."

"You are looking mighty fine to me. So fine that if I didn't have a fiancée you'd be in trouble. Line's open y'all," Tre said.

I managed a giggle, and yes I was flirting right back with Tre. So far not one call. We broke for commercial and then Tre put on a tune. Slowly one by one those lines lit up. We were in business.

"Tell the truth, girl," one listener said. "You ain't hungry all the time?"

"I used to be," I answered honestly. "But that's because I didn't want to snack on rice cakes or those little baby carrots. Before I started this diet my idea of a snack was McDonald's."

"And what you goin' do with all those clothes you can't fit into?" another asked. "Clothes are expensive."

"I'll donate them to charity unless you want me to give you some?" I swear it just slipped out.

"Shh!" Quen nudged my ankle with the tip of his leather sneakers. Tre was having a hard time trying not to crack up. But damn, what kind of stupid question was that?

"You said you started off wearing a size twenty-two. What size are you wearing now?" another caller asked.

"I'm a size eighteen," I said, "just like my age."

This time Tre burst out laughing.

The next caller was a man and he directed his question to Quen. It went on like this for the next fifteen minutes.

Almost at the end of the session, a classy female voice I swore I recognized, but maybe I was paranoid, asked, "Earlier you mentioned you'd always been heavy and your weight was something that made you feel safe. Why after all these years do you want to lose your safety net?"

Quen's jaw muscle worked so I knew he and I were on the same wavelength. Joya!

"Safe isn't always good. Sometimes you need to be challenged to realize your full potential," I said to the caller, although she hadn't identified herself. "At some point we all have to venture out of our comfort zone. You want to feel good about yourself."

"I couldn't have said that better," Quen said breaking in because he probably didn't trust me to stay calm. "What's that expression? If you keep doing what you're doing, you'll keep getting what you're getting. When you shed a few pounds it's amazing how much more energy you have and how much better you feel."

"Amen," Tre added. "Well thank you Quen Abrahams, owner of the nutrition company, Eat for Life. Thank you Chere Adams for being such a wonderful guest. In a few weeks WARP will check in on Chere's progress and hear what dress size she's wearing then. We need to pay our bills y'all. Hang with me while we go to commercial."

We were done. Quen stood up and I joined him.

"How did we do?" I asked Tre.

"You guys were off the chain."

We thanked him for having us on. Quen took my hand and together we left the studio.

"You rocked, sugar," he said when we were out in the parking lot. He held his hand out, palm up waiting for my keys.

I actually felt shy. Imagine that? And I damn near

died when Quen folded me into his arms and gave me a great big hug.

"That's for handling yourself well when Joya called in," he said.

I'd been right on the money. It had been Joya who'd asked the question about why I'd decided to lose weight after all of this time.

I doubted that the question had been prompted by any real interest in me. The good thing was I was onto her now. And if Joya Hamill knew what was good for her she would not mess with Chere Adams.

I still had street in me and I would take her down if I had to.

Chapter 14

I had been voted valedictorian. Can you believe that? Me. And I'd worked on my speech like crazy with a little help from Jen. I needed it. So there I was on the podium in front of what was left of my class with water in my eyes and a frog in my throat.

"I stand before you to tell you that all things are possible," I said. "I signed up for this class because I wanted to improve myself and there were a couple of things holding me back." I held up a hand, ticking off on my fingers. "Number one, I had a weight problem so I decided to work on that. Number two,

I needed to get a better job and I needed to learn to communicate. Most people who are somebody don't speak Ebonics."

That got a laugh. Encouraged, I continued, sounding more confident.

"This has been one bumpy journey. What I have learned is that people judge you on appearance and the way you speak. It may not happen overnight but there are benefits to investing in you. In only the short space of a few weeks I have become more confident as a person and more determined than ever to get ahead. I am not going to let anything hold me back. I want to thank Mr. Cummings for bringing us along. Let's put our hands together and give it up for our teacher, Mr. Cummings."

There was a huge applause and a few whoops and hollers from the homies who'd made it. I stepped from behind the raised platform, and the small graduating class; there were only twelve of us left cheered.

"Speech! Speech! Speech!" Everyone chanted as a red-faced Mr. Cummings made his way to the front.

He used some words I'd have to look up later while his students toasted him with cider. I stuck to diet coke. I was now on a serious diet.

At the end of the celebration, everyone promised to stay in touch. I knew no one would. After giving everyone one of my cards, I left.

I was climbing into my minivan when my cell phone rang. I didn't recognize the number.

"Hello, this is Chere."

"Hi, Chere. I'm calling because we'd said we'd have a drink sometime."

Joya! I already knew what was up with that. This wasn't just some friendly invitation or an effort to be nice.

"When did you have in mind?" I asked, curiosity taking over.

"How about right now? Are you available?"

Now was as good a time as any while I was in a relatively positive frame of mind. Might as well know what I was up against. I suggested we meet at the Haul Out.

"I'd prefer someplace less loud where we can actually sit and talk? I'd say the Pink Flamingo except there's bound to be interruptions."

I suggested another place on the boardwalk. That wasn't good enough.

"No, I've always hated that hole in the wall," Joya said, making it sound like the bar was well beneath her.

So I gave up and let her choose. She must have some place in mind.

"What about the bar at the Flamingo Beach Resort and Spa?" she came back with.

Expensive. From what I heard a drink cost ten dollars and you weren't talking about premium liquor, either. If I stuck to diet coke or water with lemon it might not be so bad.

"Okay, I'll see you in a few," I said and hung up.

I'd never set foot inside the hotel before and the lobby intimidated me. It had coral marble floors and fake palm trees that almost touched the domed glass ceilings. There were huge porch swings that had coral-and-blue striped cushions that served as seats. Colorful umbrellas were positioned over hammocks. I expected a cabana boy to pop out of someplace any minute with drinks in his hand.

There were people everywhere, some dressed like they were heading for dinner. Must be a convention from out of town because none I recognized. A bar off to the side held businessmen who craned their necks when some hot babe went by. On the opposite side, was an upscale coffee shop with Internet access. And straight ahead of me was another bar, even fancier than the first and decorated like a huge sailboat.

I headed for that bar, guessing that would be where Joya waited. A man who must be the host blocked me from entering. He was wearing navy long pants and a white shirt with those things on the shoulders. And he wore a cap like a captain wore.

"Madam, are you a guest?" he asked.

Madam? Another first for me. I didn't notice him stopping anyone else asking that question.

"I'm here to meet someone," I answered

"This is a closed party," he sniffed. "For the medical sales convention. This bar is reserved for the convention's cocktail party."

"I see."

I moved off.

"There's a bar in the spa and two outdoor ones looking over the ocean," he called after me.

I left the area and hurried outdoors. The sun had gone down and the area was artificially lit. Thin women in skimpy clothes sauntered by. I saw lots of strapless dresses and swirling skirts, hip hugging capris and really short shorts. Everywhere there were plenty of bare midriffs. Men were chatting up women and everyone seemed to be having a good time.

And here I was down to a size eighteen dress, wearing this shapeless black muumuu that I'd graduated in. I'd cheated and jazzed it up with orange mules and a necklace bearing flowers but I still didn't feel very pulled together.

I entered the first bar which had an open view of the water. There were more bright colored umbrellas with people sitting under them.

"Over here, Chere!" Joya called from a table with high stools you would have to heave yourself up onto. A man was chatting her up who must be one of the conventioneer's because I sure as heck hadn't seen him before.

When I approached they made room for me. The man wasn't exactly tall but he was in good shape and broad-shouldered.

"Is this the friend you're waiting for?" he asked, smiling at me.

"Yes, this is Chere Adams."

"Matthew Wilson." He bobbed his head and then gazed adoringly at Joya, who was sipping a green drink.

With some effort I managed to climb onto one of those high stools. I sat for at least five minutes while they continued to chat. Joya, give her her due, did try to include me in the conversation. Matthew, on his way to the cocktail party, handed Joya his business card and took off.

"You need an appletini," Joya said waving to the waitress. "Unless there's something else you prefer."

Boy was I tempted. In a fancy place like this there had to be a piña colada with my name written on it. No, no, I had to check myself. If I wanted to look like the woman across from me in the cropped white linen pants that skimmed her ankles and the aqua halter top fitting smoothly across her stomach, I needed self-control.

"I'll have a spritzer," I said.

"Boring. She'll have an appletini," Joya said to the waitress who'd just approached.

"A spritzer, please."

"No, an appletini for the lady."

The waitresses head ping-ponged back and forth. "Which will it be?

"Spritzer."

"Appletini."

"Okay, appletini," I agreed because she'd worn me down. An appletini would be my dessert. I'd never had a fancy drink like that one and it might be nice to try something new.

I could get use to this life; a life that didn't have Colt in it. Joya was busy checking out people at the bar.

"It's just tourists," she said. "The snowbirds are still down. Why is it when people vacation in Florida it becomes an excuse to break out their wild and wacky clothes?"

I liked her sense of humor. I guess my clothing could have been considered wacky before Jen took me in hand and convinced me to ditch the zebra stripes and leopard's skin. And yes, they might be in style, but on a thick person they looked like bedding.

My appletini arrived. I sucked down half of the concoction refusing to think of the calories. Gawd did that drink taste good.

"Want another?" Joya asked, egging me on.

"Sure." In less than half an hour my diet was already shot. She signaled for the waiter and told him to bring us another. I was already wondering who would drive us home.

We talked about a bunch of stuff, though to tell you the truth we had little in common.

I was on my fourth appletini, at least I think it was four, I'd lost count.

"So what's up with you and Quen?" Joya asked

I'd been expecting something like this, and even prepared my own little speech. I'd convinced myself that if she had to ask about us, that meant she was nervous. Still…

Anyway, I kept my face serious and pretended that I didn't know what she was talking about.

"Me and Quen? He's my personal trainer," I answered, making my eyes round.

"You've been out a couple of times and you work out together. And you did that interview on WARP. Quen was very open about you being his poster child."

"Quen's good people," I said and watched her expression.

Joya looked all mooney-eyed.

"Yes he is."

"Then why did you divorce him?" I was sick to death of dancing around the issue and figured might as well just put it right out there.

"We were young and inexperienced. I wanted things my way. He wanted them his. Then there was the matter of the baby we lost." She grew all serious and seemed to drift off.

"Couldn't you compromise?" I asked.

"Like I said before, we were both stubborn and very young. Compromise wasn't something in my vocabulary. I wanted it all."

A huge admission. She was willing to shoulder fifty percent of the blame for a marriage that had fallen apart. I just had to ask and needed to know.

"Do you regret leaving Quen?"

"Regret might not be the right word. Neither of us liked the idea of throwing the towel in."

"You think it's too late to salvage the relationship?" I asked, my stomach fluttering. Damn those appletinis. I watched to see her reaction.

Joya screwed up her face thinking about it for a moment. "We'll see what happens. The rest is up to Quen."

I didn't like her answer one bit.

"Maybe you should be straight up with Quen and just tell him how you feel," I said. And if she did I'd scratch her eyes out.

She sipped on her appletini gazing into the green liquid as if it were crystal ball. "I will when the time is right."

I didn't like the fact that Joya might have designs on my man. Given they'd once been married that gave her a jump-start. No way was I backing off and leaving Quen to her.

I didn't say anything for a long time.

Out of the blue, Joya asked, "Do you have feelings for Quen?"

I choked on what was left of my drink and ended up having a coughing fit. She patted me on the back.

"Are you okay?"

"Yes, thanks. Feelings? What kind of feelings? We're friends."

"Romantic feelings. He's taken you out a couple of times."

This was getting way too personal. Joya was fishing and I didn't like the idea of being grilled.

A woman cleared her throat behind me.

"Chere?" Jen eyed my glass, frowning. "Just how many drinks have you had?"

I stared at her glassy-eyed. "What are you doing here?" My tongue felt heavy.

"I'm waiting for Tre. He's taping. Who's this?"

I introduced Jen to Joya.

The two women sized each other up.

"You're the woman engaged to D'Dawg," Joya said, shaking Jen's hand. Considering she'd been out of town for a while she was very well informed. How much did she really know about my friendship with Quen?

Jen flashed her diamond with the princess setting at her. It made me envious.

"That's quite the rock," Joya said, examining Jen's hand and carefully admiring the stone.

Jen took her hand back. Her attention fixed on me again. "Trust me, I earned every carat. Young lady is this official fall off the wagon night?" She eyed my drink again.

"Oh, give her a break. It's only one night," Joya added.

I sensed the wheels turning in Jen's head. She was trying to assess the situation.

"Want to join us?" I asked.

"Maybe another time." Tre wrapped an arm around his fiancée's waist and said, "The interview went well. The exposure should drive more business to the resort."

After more introductions, and a final whispered reminder from Jen to cut back on the drinks, they took off.

"He is definitely hot," Joya said, fanning herself when they were out of earshot.

"Yup. Jen snagged a good one. He used to be the biggest player in town. She settled him down."

I was talking way too much and all because of those appletinis.

Joya's eyes went wide. "There are so few professional men around, I'd imagine Tre would attract women like hotcakes. In a lot of ways he reminds me of Quen."

I started to feel slightly queasy. All that sweet, sticky green liquid was rumbling around in my stomach.

"Quen's not a player?"

Joya tossed me this smug smile.

"Trust me, girlfriend, he is. You'd never seen that side of him because he isn't interested in you."

That sobered me up quickly. Size eighteen was now determined to take on size two.

Chapter 15

Four days later I was standing on a scale, replaying in my head what Joya had said to me about Quen being a player. I'd never heard any woman refer to him as a dog because he was a real gentleman. Joya had made that comment just to let me know I was nothing special. It hurt.

"You're up a pound, sugar," Quen said.

Yikes! How did that happen? I'd been existing on next to nothing after the appletini incident. I'd been watching every single thing I put into my mouth. To compete with Joya I would have to lose weight, and I planned on doing so quickly.

When I got off the scale Quen said, "I've been thinking that you and I should start jogging in the mornings. Usually I do so a few times a week just to change things up a bit. It would mean you getting up even earlier in the morning."

"Sure, I'll jog," I said eagerly. I wasn't about to miss out on an opportunity to spend more time with him. "And what about you cooking for me or giving me recipes or something? You promised."

I'd been feeling ignored and used ever since that evening when we'd made love. Since then Quen had stuck strictly to business.

"I'm one step ahead of you," he said. "I've been cooking up a storm all weekend. I'll drop the meals off at your place later. Everything's been weighed and every calorie accounted for. I even have labels on each container. You know, Monday, Tuesday, Wednesday. Breakfast and lunch."

"You and I are all right then?" I asked, because I was feeling insecure and needed reassurance.

"Of course we are, sugar. I'll see you later." Quen high-fived me.

He was back to treating me like I was his little

sister again. Now that Joya was back in town everything would change if I let it.

I told Quen what time I would be home and then I headed over to the *Chronicle.* We were working out of the office today and I needed to talk to Jen about that raise. It was time I started looking for my own place. I now had a taste of luxury living and was hoping to find a deal in one of the new buildings; something that I could buy with creative financing.

Jen looked up from her keyboard and nodded in my direction. "Morning."

She was normally there before I arrived and I left her there when I went home.

"Morning," I grunted back before flopping into my chair. I noisily rummaged through my bag for the carrots in Ziploc I planned on having for breakfast.

"You're snacking already?" Jen glanced at me as I gobbled down a carrot.

"Not snacking, this is breakfast."

"Which means you'll be hungry all day and cheating like crazy by dinner time."

"I don't plan on having dinner."

"What!" Jen's attention was now fully on me. She swiveled her chair. "Perhaps we should talk."

I chewed noisily on another carrot waiting for her to say something, anything.

"Your body is going to need fuel to keep it going," she lectured. "Dieting doesn't necessarily mean starving yourself. Have you discussed this crash diet with Quen?"

Quen wasn't my father. I didn't need his permission. "I'm seeing him tonight," I admitted. "And no, I did not tell him what I was doing."

"You should. By the way, you seemed really happy the other evening at Mario's. Tre and I were saying we're really glad you two are dating."

Dating? Funny but I'd never thought of me and Quen as dating. We'd hooked up. Now I was afraid to give our friendship a name.

"What did you think of Joya?" I asked.

Jen didn't answer right off but that could mean a number of things. "She seems okay," she said at last.

"What aren't you saying?"

"Doesn't it strike you as strange that she found you of all people to befriend?"

Should my feelings be hurt? Was she insulting me?

Jen continued, "Joya's just gotten back to town after being gone several years. She somehow managed to sublet one of Quen's apartments and there's not a thing he can do about it because there's no clause in the lease addressing second party renting. She's probably heard that Quen's been spending a lot of time with you. And yes, I know you two have this diet and exercise thing worked out, but he's going over and above his professional obligation. It's clearly obvious he has an interest in you."

It wasn't that obvious to me. In the back of my mind I was still thinking of myself as a booty call.

"You give any thought to my raise?" I asked, switching the subject. Hearing Joya's name always made me feel inadequate.

Jen glanced at her watch. "How's the daily quota coming? If you can maintain that we'll talk in a week."

It was better than a flat out no. Refusing to acknowledge a stomach that was beginning to speak to me in tongues, I began reading letters.

Come lunchtime though, I thought I would faint. By then I'd eaten enough crackers and drank enough water to bloat. Someone told me the combination gave you a false sense of being full. Full I wasn't but I ate one scoop of tuna fish and a measly apple, anyway.

By dinnertime I was in a downright nasty mood and feeling light headed. As I dragged myself home I decided to stay positive. In an hour or so I would see Quen, and if I was smart I'd make our time work for me.

When my doorbell rang, I was showered and dressed in another black getup. This linen dress came down to my ankles and had slits on the side. It made me look slimmer. I clipped on turquoise earrings—I missed having color, and went off to answer.

With a smile on my face I opened the door. Across the hall, Ida Rosenstein, who'd been one of the building's first tenants, was having a smoke. She didn't care, or couldn't read the huge signs declaring the building a smokefree environment. Ida made her own rules and because she was old and hard of hearing, no one had the heart to turn her in.

"You two have something going?" she barked loud enough for everyone on the floor to hear. Sure enough the door of 5D pushed open and that nosey bitch, Camille Lewis, stuck out her head.

"Told you the two of them were involved," she said in her loud Caribbean accent.

That was my signal to wave Quen in, mutter "excuse me" to Ida, and slam the door in the pot stirrer's face.

Quen carried a shopping bag in one hand, the other he held behind his back. When he set down the paper bag on the kitchen counter, he held out a bouquet of sunflowers to me.

"Here's a little something," he said. "It's my way of saying just how proud I am of you."

Not a word would come out of my mouth. No man had ever brought me flowers before. Finally I managed to mumble, "Thanks."

I clutched the sunflowers that were tied together by a violet bow in one hand and sniffled. I hoped I didn't embarrass myself by doing something stupid like getting all emotional over a gift that most women expected.

How could Quen possibly be proud of me? I'd gained weight not lost it. And I'd screwed up big time. I should have read the fine print of his rental contract and made sure there was something in there that addressed subletting. But then wasn't I sort of subletting myself? The difference was Jen and I had no signed formal agreement. She just moved in with Tre and let me rent her furnished apartment. Cheaply I might add.

I sniffled again and then thanked Quen.

"The least I could do, sugar," he said. "You hungry?"

"A little."

He should only know I could eat an entire hog right about now. I'd set the dining room table with pretty dishes Jen had bought at one of those pricey upscale stores; Crate and Tub or something like that, just in case Quen decided to stay. I hadn't been sure whether stopping by meant he was dropping off food or eating with me.

"Do you need me to heat up anything?" I offered.

"No. Tonight's dinner is all ready to go. I'll dish it out."

I felt this warm glow in the pit of my stomach. My mood immediately improved and I wasn't as light-headed as before.

Containers started coming out of Quen's bag, lots of them. Some he stacked in Jen's refrigerator. And although I didn't know what they contained, my mouth was watering. I was ready to eat.

We were down to a pitiful few bowls when Quen said, "Come on, sugar, sit down."

I sank into the chair he held out. I wasn't used to this treatment. No one ever waited on me hand and foot. The men I'd been with weren't gentlemen, though some of them claimed to be. There'd been no tenderness and no real connection between me and them.

Quen poured a yellowish liquid into a bowl. I hate to tell you what it reminded me of.

"What's that?" I asked, making a face.

"Broth. Chicken broth."

It looked like stuff they served in hospitals. I

wanted soup with noodles and dumplings, something that stuck to the ribs and filled you up.

Quen dished up a smelly piece of fish onto my plate. Next to it he placed some long green stems. I wanted a potato, rice, macaroni and cheese or buttered bread.

"Salmon and asparagus tips," Quen explained.

Yuck! Where were the pork chops, sweet potatoes and greens?

As I sat facing him I made myself eat. The soup that I had made fun of was delicious, and the salmon and asparagus much tastier than I'd expected. I was starving. I washed the whole thing down with water and a twist of lemon and pretended it was sweet tea. When I was done eating I dreamed of the dessert I just knew was coming.

Quen served up sliced strawberries and these little oranges. My mouth had been set on red velvet cake. The good thing was that now having eaten I actually felt good.

"You're an excellent cook. How did you learn?" I asked, meaning it as a compliment. I was hoping the flattery might get me at least another serving of one of those dishes he'd put in the refrigerator.

"I watched my mother when I was growing up," Quen answered. "She wasn't a healthy cook but everything was delicious. We all grew up overweight because everything was drowned in sauce and gravy. When the health problems started surfacing I figured there had to be a better way. I started getting into exercise and diet and I started experimenting by cooking my own meals. When you have a sister pass on it stays with you."

"You must still miss her," I said quietly.

"Very much. There's not a day that goes by that I don't think of Vaughn. And when you smile it's like seeing her again. You both could light up a dark room with your smiles."

"That must mean I am cute," I joked, hoping that the sad expression in Quen's chocolate eyes would go away.

"Not just cute, sugar, hot!"

I couldn't meet his eyes. Quen always made me feel good. Right now I felt like I was the most beautiful woman on Flamingo Beach. I got up and began collecting the dishes. Quen followed suit, ignoring me when I protested.

"About the other evening," he said as we stashed the plates and utensils in the dishwasher.

I held my breath. Here it came, I was about to be dumped.

"What about the other evening?"

"Wouldn't you say we let the mood take us away."

"No I wouldn't say."

Quen made sure the last plate was in the machine before closing the door. He dried his hands and reached for my shoulders. "The sex was good. Probably the best I've ever had."

"It was great sex and we should do it again." I smiled at him half joking but I meant every word.

The tips of his fingers dug into my shoulders. He'd gone all serious again.

"I don't want to hurt you."

"How could you hurt me?"

Those brown eyes were melting me, making me all gooey.

"I'm your trainer," Quen said. "You're paying me to help get you in shape. I shouldn't be taking advantage."

"Take advantage of this," I said, lifting my dress over my head and standing there in my new sexy underwear that Jen insisted I buy. I crooked a finger at Quen.

"You are too much, sugar," Quen said, moving slowly toward me, a gleam in his eye.

The next thing we were clawing each other and clothes were flying. This time we made it to the bedroom and barely to bed. Between the heavy breathing and throaty gasps we were poking around and feeling sensitive parts.

I was kneading Quen's muscles and stroking his skin and while I was doing that, I was thinking, girlfriend you need to lose weight. I wanted him to be proud of me, to walk down the street with me on his arm and a smile on his face. And then it came to me I could do it with the help of diet pills.

Meanwhile, Quen was making me happy in places I didn't think it would be possible to ever be happy again. He was loving me with his tongue and fingers. He was suckling my breasts while moving his fingers in and out of me, and I was loving every moment of it.

I wanted him inside of me; wanted to feel every lengthy inch of him. And I let him know it.

"In a minute, sugar."

Quen shifted me onto my back and got on his haunches. His hands stroked my body heating me up. I wanted to scream like a kettle. My bottom half was ripe and moist in all the right places, my body was pulsating like a live wire.

Quen parted my thighs. The tip of his tongue shot me into orbit. I twitched, spasmed and twitched again when he entered me. I was already at a place where nothing else mattered. I tuned into the sensations. I reveled in the touch and feel of Quen, the smell of citrus, the slip and slide of him entering and leaving. I relished the feeling of his rough palms on my skin and the sound of his heavy breathing.

"Quen!"

He gave one last thrust and that did it. I was over the edge.

"I love you," I said.

His muscles bunched underneath my hands and on a deep sigh he came.

For a long time afterward we lay still. I thought Quen might have fallen asleep until his cell phone jingled.

"Do you need to get that?" I whispered.

Groan then finally, "Nah. That's what voice mail is for."

His response sort of made up for him not telling me he loved me back, but not totally. Another few minutes went by before he got up and began dressing. In the back of my mind I wondered if we were just doomed to be sex buddies.

"What about running tomorrow?" he asked, when we were out in the kitchen and he was packing up his empty containers.

"Sure. What time?"

"Early. I'm thinking five-thirty. If you're game I'll

meet you in the lobby. Since you're just starting out we'll take it easy. Wear something comfortable and loose, and get yourself a pair of good running sneakers."

We were back to business again.

I nodded. Did I have a choice?

Quen's cell phone jingled again. He dug through his pockets, got out his flip phone, glanced at the number and put the phone to his ear.

"Yes, Joya?"

I tuned in shamelessly to the one sided conversation.

"Hmm, Peter and Dustin took the keys to New York with them?" Quen glanced in my direction. "Sure I can get a key to you. Tonight? Uh, that might be a problem."

It was going on ten the last time I looked. Joya had to have known that Quen was out and she had his number.

"What's so urgent that you need to get into the apartment tonight... Who's helping you move your things? And they're only available now... I see. Okay, I'll leave them at the front desk with the security guard."

I exhaled the breath I didn't know I was holding. My relief was short-lived.

"You were hoping I'd meet you at the condo…walk through a one-bedroom apartment?"

Quen rolled his eyes. I rolled mine back at him.

"Pick up the keys at the front desk," he said and disconnected.

"I need to pay you for the food," I said, getting my purse.

"Tonight's meal is on me. I'll invoice you for the rest."

Quen gave me a tight hug and kissed the top of my head. I could tell he was distracted and wanted out in a hurry.

I thought about what we'd just done; made love like only two people who cared about each other could. But I wanted to be more than a booty call.

I wanted Quen to look at me like Tre looked at Jen.

Chapter 16

Yeah! I was down to a size sixteen dress and it had only taken a month or so to get there. The good thing was I no longer felt hungry. My over-the-counter diet pills were working. I popped one of those buggers in my mouth and zap I had energy, or at least I felt like I did.

Energy enough that I was exercising twice a day. Right now I was out on the boardwalk with my hand weights. I planned on speed walking. I was feeling especially good because I'd sold another condo and I had the nice fat commission check in hand.

I could make my monthly car payment to Dickie Dyson without sweating and didn't have to worry about him looking to collect more than money. I'd also gotten a lead on a condo I might be able to buy. Jen hadn't said another word about me moving out. She still couldn't make up her mind whether she was selling or renting. Either way I couldn't afford what she was asking.

I'd been lucky to run into Ida Rosenstein in the elevator a few days back. She'd given me an ear load about a friend whose family was putting her in an assisted living facility. Ida's friend wasn't quite ready to give up her condo, being that she'd been in the building almost as long as Ida but she would consider a lease with option to buy when she was ready. Part of the rent would go to the down payment.

I'd said I might be interested in a lease with option to buy, although I didn't have a clue where I would get the money. So now I was hoping Ida could put in a good word for me and I could swing it. It would be the ideal situation all around, especially since the old lady had one of those corner apartments with a great view of the beach and boardwalk. Even if it was a bit musty I could air it out and slap on a coat of paint. And I would be living high on the hog.

The sun was going down and several evening

joggers zoomed by me. Preparing to walk, I put my head back and thrust out my chest. My six pound weights felt heavy but I was determined to complete the two mile walk which was the personal goal I'd set for myself.

Quen and I had gone jogging that morning as well. I hadn't mentioned that I was doubling up on the exercising. He'd been complimentary about my appearance and proud as heck of the weight I'd lost. He'd assumed it was because of the diet he'd put me on and I didn't want to pull the rug out from under him. The truth of the matter was that the diet pills killed my appetite and made me zing.

I was so focused on walking briskly that I didn't see the cyclist until she was almost on top of me.

"Chere is that you?"

I recognized the voice but almost didn't recognize the tiny woman perched on a bicycle wearing a cap with the brim pulled low over her eyes.

"Hey, you," I said back.

Joya had stopped peddling. She was wearing a grin a mile wide.

"Looks like you're working up a sweat. Can I interest you in dinner? I was thinking of heading for the pizza joint. A pizza and a cold beer could be exactly what the doctor ordered."

Although I no longer had an appetite I was tempted. It seemed like months since I'd had a Colt and even longer since I'd had pizza. I was also curious to find out what she wanted. I hadn't run into her on the boardwalk before, it seemed strange I would run into her now.

"Oh, come on, live a little," Joya said, "I'll drive. How about I pick you up in front of your building in half an hour?"

How did she know where I lived? Then again everyone knew everything in Flamingo Beach. She must have seen me coming out of Jen's building. Curiosity got the best of me. Quen had been very close mouthed after that phone call, and I had no idea what was going on between the two of them. Not that I would take Joya's word as gospel.

"Okay," I said. "Half an hour should give me time to clean up."

"Great, see you then."

Joya peddled away looking young and carefree. I'd heard from the beauty shop crowd who knew even more than me, that she was my age. Thirty-three.

After she disappeared out of sight I cut my walk short and doubled back. I was determined to take a quick shower and climb into decent clothes. I couldn't have Joya showing me up.

At the appointed time I was showered, changed and downstairs in front of the building.

Joya pulled up in a sporty red BMW, tooting her horn just in case anyone missed her. The car had a black interior and was a convertible. The top was down and Ms. Thang was wearing a white halter top and her Jada Pinkett Smith sunglasses in red that matched the car.

I shouldn't have wasted my time agonizing. Size sixteen just couldn't compete with size two. I'd thought I was cute in my black walking shorts—my new color—and a long beige T-shirt that hid my hips.

I forced a smile and got into the front seat. No sooner had I done that, Joya sped off. The good folks of Flamingo Beach stared at us as we zipped through Main Street, passing the historical district and Joya's grandmother's store Joya's Quilts. We'd be the topic of every dinner conversation tonight and there would be a lot of speculation.

"How are you settling in?" I asked to be polite and because I was in the front seat of her car.

"I'm loving the apartment I'm renting. I don't have a lot of stuff but I have the essentials."

"That's nice. You gotta love the view."

"It's great. How do you know about my view?"

I gave her a sideways look. "I rented that apartment to Peter and Dustin. Initially they were going to buy but didn't want to spring for a water view. Aren't they who you're subletting from?"

She got really quiet. "Yes."

"So how come I haven't seen a lot of you?' I asked. "You must be helping your grandmother out in the quilt shop during the day?"

"Actually, no." Joya took a sharp left and sent me flying against the door. "Sorry. I'm managing the Vintage Place."

"Come again?"

"Carlton's liquor store changed hands it has a new name. Peter and Dustin Millard are the new owners and they've got big plans for the place. It's being turned into a wine and cheese shop complete with wine tastings. I'm managing the store temporarily until the guys can wrap up their business in New York."

I had to give the woman credit. She'd been here only a couple of weeks and had managed to find an apartment with a to-die-for view and a job some would kill for. It would be only a matter of time before she found herself a man, if she hadn't already. My man.

"I'd say you settled in quite well. Will the airline hold your job indefinitely?"

Joya took her eyes off the road for a brief second. "I took a six month leave of absence with the understanding I could extend it if I needed more time.

"Time for what?"

"To find myself."

A peculiar answer and too damn new age for me.

We were on the side street now where Castiglione's Pizza was. The Italian family had owned the shop for years, at least they been there since I moved to town. And there were dozens of them who regardless of being male or female looked alike. Most of the men and two of the women had married outside their race. I think it might have something to do with the fact that there weren't a lot of white single young people in Flamingo Beach. As the demographics shifted most whites fled further north. But black, white or mocha, the Castigliones looked like each other.

Joya parked her Beemer and we entered the restaurant together. A few families were still finishing up dinner and a handful of teenagers sat at the Formica counters snacking and talking about how bad life was in general. They should get to be my age.

"Whatcha havin'?" Joey Castiglione, asked slamming the oven door and approaching the counter. His hands were coated in flour and his dark curly hair was threaded in silver. There were no other Castigliones around.

I'd once had a thing for Joey but it never went anywhere. I think I might have reminded him of his mother because of my size. He didn't seem to recognize me now.

"Hey, Joey," I said. "How you been?"

His hair sticking up in clumps, and a dusting of flour on his cheeks, he stared at me for a moment then finally said, "Chere Adams. What happened to you?"

"I lost weight."

He kept staring at Joya.

"The hot-looking woman with you must be Joya Abrahams."

Joya flashed him one of those smiles that made smart men go stupid. Joey turned abruptly and rammed into a pile of trays. They clattered to the floor. He used the excuse of picking them up to gather his composure.

"Hamill, right? You took back your maiden name," he said when he straightened. I'd never seen Joey this red.

"I did," Joya said tapping her cheek for Joey's

floury kiss. "Hey, Joey, do you think you can make us a pizza with the works? I'd like extra cheese please and sausage. And we'll have two Coors."

"Coming right up."

Joey gave me a kiss, too, but I could tell he was doing it to be polite.

"Where would you ladies like to sit?" he asked.

We looked around for a spot and Joey began sweeping trash off the tables and into a garbage bag. He wiped down the tabletops with a cloth tied around his middle.

"What about over there?" Joya said, pointing to a table for two in the corner.

"You got it."

The table was ready before we even walked over. The Castigliones were from the Bronx like me, and they still moved with whirlwind speed. That pizza was done in record time. Some poor bugger who called in for delivery was going to have to wait.

Joya and I sat across from each other. Joey kept staring at me as if he still couldn't believe what he saw. He was particularly fascinated by my legs and couldn't seem to take his eyes off them. I'd worn a miniskirt; the only thing I could fit into now that didn't look like I'd borrowed it from an aunt.

"Damn, you've shrunk, girl," Joey repeated over and over. I wanted to slap that silly grin off his face. He left to fetch our beer and I concentrated on how good the pizza smelled. I wasn't starving but pizza is pizza.

Joey was back. He plunked down two bottles and a couple of plastic cups. Joya poured her beer into a cup making sure there wasn't a head. She touched her plastic cup against my bottle.

"To friends," she said, looking me in the eye. "What's with you and Quen?"

I tried to keep a straight face and not give anything away. But her question really shook me up. I took a swig of beer. I hadn't had alcohol since the appletinis and that one gulp went straight to my head.

"Quen's my personal trainer and my nutritionist. What's it to you?"

"You spend a lot of time together."

"So?"

"So, it gives people the impression that there's more going on than just you two working out. Is there?"

I took a large mouthful of beer. "Would that be a problem for you?" I asked.

Joya looked at me with those huge gray eyes of

hers. "Not exactly a problem, but there are a couple of things you need to know about Quen."

"Like what?" I pushed the half-drunk bottle of beer away and put my elbows on the table. I was beginning to feel queasy.

"Like I still love him."

"You're divorced," I said bluntly.

"That might be so and I take full responsibility. It was a bad move on my part. We had our issues. I wanted to make him into something he was not. I wanted to fix him."

"I can't imagine Quen needed fixing," I said dryly.

"He didn't but I did."

Joey returned with our pizza on a round tray. He set it down in the center of the table and slapped down two plates.

"Enjoy," he said before racing off to take care of another table.

Joya used a knife to separate the pieces. She plopped a huge slice on my plate then placed a smaller slice on the plate in front of her. She nibbled delicately while I took a huge bite.

"You were saying?" I asked with my mouth full.

"No, you were saying you didn't think Quen needed fixing."

“I don’t think any man needs fixing. You accept what you get and work with it a little.”

“Hmm. I don’t know if I necessarily agree. Quen and I were young hopefuls. I saw his potential but he didn’t. He was content to spend his time in T-shirt and track shorts. I thought it was a waste. I wanted so much more for him.”

“A waste to work with people?”

“No, a waste of his potential, period. How much could he possibly make as an exercise guru?”

I bit into my pizza finding it looked better than it tasted, and Joey did make a good pizza. I’d lost my appetite and nothing tasted as good as it looked.

“I thought personal trainers did okay,” I said. “They charge a hefty hourly rate.” She didn’t need to know that Quen was discounting his normal hourly rate for me.

“Okay is relative. Young couples need money. I had student loans. We had rent, car payments, new furniture that wasn’t paid for, a baby on the way that we lost. We needed to be practical.”

She’d painted a different picture for me. Most people made it sound like Joya was selfish, and that she’d kept pushing Quen to become something he was not.

I took another bite of pizza. It was something to do and felt comforting.

"Why are you telling me this?" I asked.

Joya nibbled on her slice. She set it back on the plate. "I don't want Quen to hurt you."

Why the hell would she care? Sounded to me like she might be worried. Like my size sixteen body was now cause for concern.

I looked Joya in the eye and said, "And you think Quen would hurt me? Why?"

"Not intentionally. He's a sweet guy and you might misunderstand his intentions."

I was starting to get mad. What did she know about anything? What gave her the right to tell me not to misinterpret Quen's interest in me? They were divorced, supposedly over. Done with. While Joya might be repeating all the things that kept me up at night I didn't need to hear it from her.

I excused myself and went to the bathroom where I promptly threw up. Too much pizza. Too much sauce. I took a few minutes to compose myself and fix my face.

Then I walked back to our table to find Joey chatting Joya up.

"We need to leave," I said to her.

"So soon? You just got here." Joey looked disappointed.

"I have someplace to be."

Joya glanced at her watch and jumped to her feet. "Shoot, I'm going to be late. I'm heading over to Quen's place to get some stuff."

"Perfect," I said. "Because that's exactly where I'm going. Why don't we walk in and surprise him together?"

Chapter 17

"You didn't seem your usual energetic self tonight, sugar," Quen said after we'd finished our third radio interview at WARP.

"I'm fine." Actually I was tired and still a little bit ticked at him. I didn't know whether Joya had been telling the truth or not because he either wasn't home or was refusing to answer his door when we'd shown up.

Quen's fingers circled my arm, turning me around. His chocolate eyes scanned my face and I heard the concern in his voice.

"Are you taking your vitamins?"

"Umm, hmm."

I was dragging, had been dragging lately and always felt slightly sick. It just didn't seem like I had energy. My heart was constantly racing and I always felt nauseous. But the good thing was that I was still losing weight, though not as much as I had hoped for.

In the parking lot, Quen stopped me from getting into the minivan.

"You in a hurry?"

"Why?"

"I thought maybe we could stop into the Pink Flamingo and get a snack. I don't know about you but I was rushing and didn't have much of a dinner."

"Okay. You want me to follow you?"

"No, leave your car. I'll drive."

I wasn't hungry but I wasn't about to pass up on an opportunity to spend time with Quen. And yes, we saw each other practically every day but most of that time was spent working out or jogging, and we hadn't had time to talk.

I'd been really upset since that night I'd had pizza with Joya. But I didn't want to come right out and ask Quen if he was seeing her. I would only sound jealous and I really didn't have any claim on the man.

He held the passenger door open and waited for me to slide into the car. My whole body zinged. I wasn't getting much sleep lately. Even Jen had commented that I looked wild eyed and edgy. She said I was losing too much weight too soon. Of course I didn't tell her about the diet pills I was taking because I really didn't want a lecture.

We drove across town in silence. Quen seemed to be preoccupied. He'd taken to complimenting me about how good I looked, or about the outfit I was wearing but tonight he said nothing. I thought I looked cute. I was wearing a halter dress in a light shade of green and beige high-heeled backless sandals, silver jewelry and makeup that made me look glamorous. Because I knew I was going to be interviewed I had driven to Jacksonville to one of the big department stores and had the woman at the cosmetic counter do my face.

We passed through the gated entrance of Flamingo Place. Quen found a parking spot at the Pink Flamingo and helped me out of the car. Holding hands, we walked into the restaurant together.

"You guys rocked tonight," Rico Catalban, the manager said, greeting us. He was referring to our interview. "I can't believe how open you were about your weight loss. People really like that because it motivates them. You're a shadow of what you used to be."

I managed to smile and thank him. Bypassing the bar, we followed him to a table. I wasn't hungry. I never seemed to be lately but I ordered a bowl of fish chowder anyway.

Quen waited for our meals to be placed in front of us before starting in on me.

"You've changed," he said, fixing me with his brown-eyed stare.

"How's that?" I raised my spoon to my lips but couldn't bring myself to taste the broth.

"You used to be peppy, straight up and to the point. Now I don't have a clue what you're thinking. What's going on?"

I tried smiling. I knew I was changing but didn't think it would be that noticeable. My goal was only to better myself and make myself more attractive to him.

"I'm reinventing myself," I answered, forcing an energy I didn't feel into my voice. "Now that I have this Realtor job I have to tone down a bit. You know, act more professional."

"Just as long as it's an act. I liked the old you. You were confident, sassy and willing to take on just about anything and anybody."

I wondered if what he said was really true that he liked the old me.

"I lugged around a lot of weight," I said. "I might have seemed confident but I wasn't happy."

"You appeared to be."

"Appearances are deceiving."

I had been comfortable buffered by all that fat. It permitted me to be funny and act as if nothing bothered me, as a fat person it was acceptable to clown around. I'd initially put on all that weight to keep men away from me, that was before I discovered the chubby chasers of the world.

"Tell the truth," I said, "People are more attracted to the skinny me."

"Not me, sugar. Is that why you're not eating?"

He'd noticed.

"No, I'm just not hungry."

Quen gave me another of his soulful looks. I'd set my spoon aside and given up trying.

He leaned across the table and covered my hand.

"I agreed to work with you because I liked you and was concerned about your health. I didn't want what happened to my sister to happen to you." Quen held up a finger before I could interrupt. "I'm worried, sugar. You're losing too much weight and all in a short space of time."

He liked me. He was concerned. That's all I focused on. I'd given this man my heart and would gladly give him my soul. I wanted to be skinny for him. It's what he liked, or at least that's what I thought he liked.

"Something's wrong," Quen probed. "You used to be a real fireplug and good with comebacks. Your over-the-top personality was what attracted me to you."

A female voice interrupted.

"Hey, Quen are we on for tomorrow?"

I looked up to see a woman whom I'd seen at the gym giving him one of those slit-eyed looks that said, "I want to lay with you." She had a toned body that shouted "gym rat." I wasn't worth her time so she ignored me.

"Yes, we have a ten o'clock session," Quen said, smiling back.

The woman stood there longer than she should, making a feeble attempt at conversation, and excluding me. Finally she left.

"I want to look just like her," I announced when she was gone.

Quen shook his head. "You can't," he said bluntly. "You're a different body type."

I wasn't sure how to take that. He was attracted

to my over the top personality? Did that mean he didn't find me pretty? I didn't need him to know how insecure I was so I refused to ask. I did need to know about Joya though.

"Has your ex been in touch with you?" I asked switching the conversation.

Quen scrunched up his nose. "Yes, she's called a couple of times primarily with questions about the apartment. How to put the lights on timers, work the Jacuzzi tub that kind of thing. She's asked me to come over to show her how to use one thing or another but I've always refused. The closest I've come is having coffee with her."

What about inviting her over to your apartment?

Quen finished up the grouper sandwich that he'd ordered and stared at the soup in my bowl.

"Sure you don't want something else, sugar?"

I shook my head. What I wanted to do was go home and fall into bed. I was so sleepy and tired. Lately my hands had taken to shaking.

Quen kept a hand on the small of my back as he steered me from the restaurant. On the way out he got flagged down by a bunch of skinny women.

"I'll see you Monday," one said

"If you're going to Tamika's party will you save a dance for me?"

"Can you work up some menus for me, Quen?"

And you wonder why I was feeling insecure and why I needed to get the weight off?

Quen drove home with one hand on the wheel and the other around my shoulders. When we got to Jen's building he walked with me to the elevator and saw me to my door. He refused to come in.

"Sorry, hon. I have a busy day ahead of me tomorrow. Remember we're meeting earlier than our normal. Five o'clock not six."

I nodded my head. I'd almost forgotten about our jogging date. I was dragging and needed my sleep. Then Quen gave me a quick kiss on the lips and hightailed it out of there.

Feeling as if I'd been abandoned, I closed and double locked the door, went into the bathroom and began stripping off clothes. Before I got into bed I set the alarm and popped another diet pill. For a long time I lay there thinking about everything Quen had said to me that evening.

Had he been real? Had I changed that much? Was it really my personality that did it for him? And in the back of my mind I couldn't help wondering if he was still in love with Joya and whether they were attempting to work things out.

I must have drifted off because the next thing I remembered was a loud noise in my ear. I rolled over, slapped off the alarm clock and dragged myself from bed. Feeling dizzy I stumbled into the bathroom and splashed water on my face but that didn't help with the queasiness.

I managed to make it out the front of my building at the specified time, just seconds before Quen came jogging up.

"Hi, sugar. Sleep well?" he asked, running in place.

I grunted. He was used to me not being talkative in the mornings. We began to stretch and bend, warming up. My thoughts were now on what I had to accomplish today. Ida's friend, the old lady was coming around and wanted to talk to me about leasing her place with option to buy. I needed to hotfoot it over there before she changed her mind.

Jen and I also had plans to work on the Sunday column. That meant she would have me reading more than my quota of letters; only the most out there ones would get published. I'd also promised Sheena to go to the movies with her later and I had paperwork yet to complete. A client had made a ridiculous offer, and it was my job to go through the motions of presenting that offer to the seller although I already knew it would be turned down.

I clapped on my headphones and Quen and I

started a slow jog toward the boardwalk. I was still foggy and I put it down to being half awake.

Few people were out and about at that hour except for the enterprising vendors getting an early start. There were the usual assortment of hawkers selling newspapers, coffee, Danish and bagels. The air off the ocean was still cool and semirevived me. I got a second wind and I jogged alongside Quen for at least ten minutes without saying a thing.

Why did I feel so sluggish and slightly out of it? Why was my heart racing and why had a knot settled in my chest? The blur ahead of me was the boardwalk slowly rising to meet my feet. I couldn't make my limbs move another inch. And although I wanted to sit down, pride got the best of me. All I remember is blackness settling in.

"Chere talk to me, say something, sugar." Quen's voice came from far away.

A hand was on my wrist, feeling for something. A high-pitched wailing filled my ears that reminded me of a kettle. Something cold clamped over my nose and mouth. The lump on my chest lifted and now I could breathe more easily. I was on a bed strapped in tight and shoved into the back of a vehicle that reminded me of a Brink's truck.

"I'm coming with her," a man's voice insisted.

My brain was scrambled. I was being taken somewhere against my will. I tried to get into a seated position but some invisible force held me back. I wanted to ask questions but even my voice failed me. I was being held captive by a force I couldn't see.

"Sugar?"

Quen's voice in my ear. His hand on mine. Blackness again.

I woke up in strange room and in a comfortable bed. I felt the quiet.

"Look who's awake," a woman in a pink dress said.

I struggled up. "Where the hell am I?"

A cool palm stroked my forehead. "You're in the hospital, love."

"How did I get here?"

The nurse filled me in. She said I'd collapsed while jogging. Quen panicked thinking it was a heart attack and called 911. I was now being kept for observation and I'd been scheduled for testing.

"I need to talk to Quen," I said. "I have a job. I'm scheduled to go into the paper today. What about my friend, Sheena, we're meeting up later? Hell, I have a bunch of things to do."

"You have nothing to do today except lie here and rest. Your boyfriend notified whoever needed to know that you were in the hospital. Our phones have been ringing off the hook and your friend's been driving the nurses and doctors crazy. He refuses to go home until he speaks with you."

"Isn't he sweet."

"You hooked a good one, lady. And trust me I have seen them all."

"Please I'd like to see him."

Seeing Quen would help reassure me I would be all right. His presence would comfort me.

"You can see your boyfriend for five minutes," the nurse said. "Let me find him." She straightened the covers on the bed and left. I didn't bother telling her Quen was not my boyfriend.

I must have drifted off because what jolted me awake was a rough palm in my hand. My eyes flew open.

"Quen!"

"How are you feeling, sugar?"

Words failed me. Were there tears in his eyes or was it just my imagination.

"What happened?" I wanted to hear it from his mouth. I trusted him.

"One moment you were jogging alongside me, the next you were on the ground," he said.

"I remember feeling weird."

"You must not be eating or taking your vitamins. What does the doctor say?"

"I don't know I haven't seen him yet."

"Hmm."

I didn't want to talk about food or the lack of it.

"Did you call Jen and let her know I wouldn't be in today?" I asked.

"It's all taken care of. You have nothing to worry about just concentrate on getting your rest."

My eyelids were heavy again. Must be the medication or whatever was dripping into my arm. Quen squeezed my hand and I squeezed his back. I closed my eyes and began to relax.

"You've had your five minutes," the nurse said bustling back in and shooing Quen out.

"No, please let him stay…"

I felt a moist kiss on my forehead. "I'll be back later, sugar."

And even though I was half asleep, I knew the minute when he left the room because I immediately felt his loss.

I had one helluva problem. I was in love with a man who didn't love me back.

Chapter 18

The next day I was still in the hospital and I was starting to get scared and frustrated. No one would tell me a thing. The standard answer was, "Let's just wait until the results of your tests come back."

Not good enough I wanted to know. If I was dying I wanted to know. Now.

Meanwhile I had a steady stream of visitors. Sheena stopped by to see what I wanted and to tell me she and Manny were still going strong. She was also going strong with Dickie Dyson. Knowing

Sheena she was getting something more substantial from these guys other than sex.

Jen came by to tell me not to worry, that she'd hired a temp from an agency to fill in and all I needed to do was concentrate on getting better. Even Ian Pendergrass came by to see how I was doing and tell me my job was secure. I might be sick but I wasn't stupid. I used that opportunity to hit him up for a raise. And I got it. Now I had gone over Luis Gomez's head.

Quen, to my surprise, stopped by on his way to work with a huge bouquet of pink roses for me. They were sitting in a black lacquer vase on the dresser. I still couldn't quite figure the guy out.

I'd finished showering and was eating a clear bowl of broth and some tasteless Jell-O when Joya came rushing in. She was carrying a card in one hand and a huge teddy bear in the other. She was the last person I wanted to see.

"I came as soon as I heard you were in the hospital," she said, plopping the fat potbelly bear in the ridiculous miniskirt, mesh stockings and platform shoes on my bed. When she squeezed the bear's paw, it began singing an old Supremes song in Diana Ross's voice. I wasn't sure whether to thank her or cry. Dressed in its ridiculous getup, the poor thing looked like me in my heavier days. If I truly had that bad fashion sense people weren't laughing with me but at me.

I managed to thank her. I had to believe Joya meant well.

She sank into the chair across from my bed. "What's the doctor saying?"

I shrugged. "I don't know yet. Not until the tests come back. The nurses say I'm supposedly undernourished."

"Then get off the diet. Trust me, thin isn't all it's cracked up to be." She laughed but her huge gray eyes were filled with compassion. When she glanced at the dresser and my roses, her expression changed.

"Who'd you get roses from?"

I took a deep breath, got myself centered and told her.

"Quen sent you flowers?"

"Yes, it's not the first time he has."

"Hmm!"

What the hell did *hmm* mean?

"How are you liking your apartment?" I asked trying to be nice and wanting to steer her off the topic.

"It suits my purposes for now."

Her eyes were on my roses again. She got out of the chair and crossed over to the dresser, staring closely at the dozen long stemmed pink roses in an expensive vase. She sniffed them and then fingered the petals.

"The card's still here," Joya said. "In the envelope."

"I never even saw it."

I'd been asleep when the flowers arrived and they'd been set down on the bureau.

She flipped the envelope at me. I caught it with shaking hands and opened the envelope.

No one's sweeter in the world than you, sugar. Get well soon. I miss you.

Quen

There was no one in the world sweeter than him.

My eyes filled with tears. They trickled down my cheeks. Joya handed me a tissue.

"You're in love with Quen, aren't you?" she said.

No point in lying it had to be written all over my face.

"Yes, I'm in love with him. He's been wonderful to me."

"Quen is very lovable and he's a romantic, too."

I had to ask. "If you feel that way why did you divorce him?"

Joya sat back down again. Her fingers pinched her chin. "I've often asked myself that very question. But the truth of the matter is we weren't very compatible. I wanted to go and see the world whereas Quen loves Flamingo Beach. It still provides him with everything he wants."

"Is that such a bad thing to love your home?"

I was thinking about the men I knew and some of the nasty things they did, like molest young children and force them to do awful things, and then warn them not to tell adults. If this was the only fault Quen had—and I didn't see it as a fault—I would take it.

Joya continued. "I wanted the best for Quen because I believe the only way we can overcome is to make something of ourselves. Education is key."

Was that a swipe she'd just taken at Quen.

"But Quen did make something of himself," I said.

"Now he has. I kept pushing him to do something outside of that gym. Get a degree in something that paid real money. He didn't do that until I left him."

It was interesting to hear Joya's side of things. What she wanted for Quen didn't seem unreasonable to me, how she went about it might have been the issue. Maybe I had misjudged her.

She stood. "You're tired and I've taken up enough of your time. Call me if you need anything." I thanked her. She surprised me by leaning over and kissing my cheek. "Take care, Chere."

She left me with a lot to think about. I held Quen's card in my hand staring at it, and trying to figure out if there was some hidden meaning behind his words. Maybe it was just the kind of note a brother would send to his sister.

Later that day Dr. Maxwell Benjamin came in to see me.

"Your results are back," he said, scrutinizing the clipboard in his hand. I held my breath waiting. "Why didn't you tell me you were taking diet pills?"

"You asked if I was taking medication. Diet pills aren't prescription drugs, at least mine aren't."

"But they do have enough caffeine in them to hot-wire a horse. You're dehydrated, undernourished and your blood pressure is way above normal."

My stomach fluttered and my hands went ice cold. "How long do I have to live?"

Dr. Benjamin looked at me, startled. He threw back his head and roared. "You've gone cold turkey for two days. Just forget the pills and you'll lessen the risk of having a heart attack or stroke. Develop good eating habits and continue to exercise."

"When can I get out of here?" I pleaded.

Dr. Ben looked at me over the top of his glasses. "We've already started pumping nutrients into you.

As soon as we can agree that you'll eat well-balanced meals and get your energy level back, you're free."

It would be worth getting off of my ridiculous diet if I could get out of the hospital today. I remembered the conversation I'd had with Quen the night after one of our third radio interviews. He'd said that it wasn't my thinner self he'd been attracted to. And here I was losing weight for all the wrong reasons; doing it more for him than for me. I'd never enjoyed being fat although I'd gotten comfortable at it.

I'd turned into this whole other person constantly worried about what I put into my mouth, concerned about what I looked like, and worried about what others thought of me. Instead of me feeling better about me, I was agonizing and pushing myself to be thin. Because I thought thin meant happy and would get me the guy I wanted.

Dr. Benjamin began giving me a stern lecture about taking care of myself and not looking for an artificial fix to my problems. If I wasn't so weak and he wasn't so good-looking I would have answered him back. Right now my primary focus was to get the hell out of the hospital, do some thinking and find me again; the me inside that larger, more comfortable shell.

* * *

Two days later I was released from the hospital. Quen was there to pick me up and was the person who drove me home. It felt good to have his arm around me as he steered me down the hallway and toward Jen's apartment. I handed him her key, and as he placed it in the lock, a door across the hallway opened. Camille Lewis stuck her head out the opening.

"I heard you were in the hospital," the nasty witch said. "You don't look so hot."

Thanks, I needed that. I still wasn't myself and didn't feel like getting into it with her, so I just smiled and said, "I'm getting better every day and thanks for caring."

Without another word, she slammed her door.

"You're back to form," Quen said, a hand on my arm, leading me into the apartment.

The moment we entered music came on.

"Surprise!"

The place was alive with people crawling out of the places they were hiding. There was Sheena, Jen, Tre and some of my girls from the office. There was Dickie, Manny, Chet Rabinowitz and Harley. Ida Rosenstein with an unlit cigarette dangling from the side of her mouth, Luis Gomez, the weasel, and even Ian had come.

Quen set down my suitcase by the door. I was embraced, squeezed, kissed and patted before finally being led to a seat. I accepted balloons and flowers. Jen gave me a beautiful silver necklace with matching earrings and handed me an envelope that I tucked into the side of my chair for safekeeping.

Someone had gone all out with the catering. There was shrimp, clams, mussels and salads of every kind. People began eating and drinking. In less than an hour they were gone.

"Let's get you to bed," Quen said, the minute the last guest had disappeared.

"Not quite yet. I want to sit on the balcony and look out at the view. I want to see the palm trees swaying and I want to smell the salt from the ocean." I was in a strange mood. The hospital had left me claustrophobic and valuing things I'd never thought much about.

I'd spent too many days lying flat on my back. Now what I wanted most was fresh air and to look out on the ocean.

"How about I get you something to eat or drink, sugar? There's plenty inside, except for ice tea you haven't touched anything."

"I'm not hungry."

I'd had breakfast before being discharged from the hospital and I was full and happy just to be with Quen. The dizzy spells were a thing of the past but I still felt drained.

Quen led me through the sliding glass doors and onto the balcony. He sat right next to me.

"We need to talk," he said.

Uh-oh. When a man said that to a woman it wasn't good. I braced myself and prepared for anything. "Sounds serious," I joked.

"It is serious. I feel responsible for you going into the hospital. I should have been more involved and been monitoring you every step of the way."

"I'm not a child."

Quen gave me a hard look. "That's obvious to me, hon. You're one gorgeous woman and therein lies the problem. If I hadn't pushed you so hard you wouldn't have gone overboard."

I wouldn't have Quen beat himself up like that. None of this was his fault.

"You weren't pushing me," I said. "You didn't open my mouth and force me to take diet pills. You encouraged me to eat healthy and in proper portions. And you went out of your way to prepare balanced meals. I'm the one who screwed everything up."

I started crying and couldn't stop. My blood sugar must be low and my hormones out of whack.

"Sugar," Quen said, sounding like he wanted to cry himself. He hugged me to him. "I've done a lot of soul-searching and truthfully I think I did you a disservice. I should have had one of my employees work with you. You reminded me too much of my sister. Your smile, your personality…the whole bit. I couldn't get beyond that."

"My size was what did it," I said, struggling to joke.

"Maybe your size, too," Quen admitted. "I was attracted to you but my emotional baggage held me back. And when you fainted, it was like déjà vu all over again. Your stint in the hospital gave me time to think about a lot of things."

"Like what?" I asked, daring to hope that he was finally seeing me as a woman, and not just the buddy that provided additional benefits.

"Like I like you too much. Like I'm no longer in love with my ex-wife and ready to move on." Quen stood and stretched. "Look, we should be having this conversation on the boardwalk with a full moon overhead, not when you're still recuperating. I'm going to knock on Jen and Tre's door and have her get you settled in." He leaned over and kissed my cheek. "I'll call you later to see how you're doing."

Then he left.

Chapter 19

The doorbell rang as I was thinking about dinner. People had been checking on me all day. I was grateful that so many cared but enough was enough. I was all talked out and now I needed my space.

Manny had flowers delivered and Dickie Dyson sent over a driver to find out if I needed anything. The whole town must be talking about how I almost died, a slight exaggeration of course. Some poster child for health and exercise I'd turned out to be.

I let the answering machine pick up the last several calls and shut off my cell phone. I was so tired by then I couldn't think much less cope with people. Now I had an unwanted visitor

I stumbled to the door and put an eye to the peephole. The figure on the other side was blurry and out of focus.

"Who is it?" I called, hoping it was a delivery person and I could tell them to set whatever it was in front of the door.

"Quen."

At the sound of his voice my entire body buzzed and unmentionable places began to pulse. Why was he back?

I opened the door and he held a shopping bag out to me. In his other hand there was a duffle; the kind people carried with a change of clothing when they were going to work out. We stood staring at each other.

"Come in," I finally said, moving aside. "What's in the shopping bag?"

"Our dinner." He gave me a hug and a moist kiss on the tip of my ear. Then he headed for the kitchen.

He was being so thoughtful, had always been that way. I could hear him unpacking the covered dishes and laying them out on the counter. The contents smelled delicious. I followed the smells to the kitchen. I must be getting my appetite back, now I just had to remember to eat in moderation.

Quen handed me a glass of something white and frothy.

"You're giving me a milk shake?"

"No, it's a protein drink."

I took a sip and pronounced it delicious.

"Where would you like to eat?" Quen asked.

It sounded to me like he was planning on staying.

"I was thinking of going to bed," I admitted.

"Then I'll bring in a tray."

I could get used to this treatment; Quen waiting on me hand and foot.

Before taking off I asked, "What's in the duffle bag?"

"Stuff."

"What do you need stuff for?"

"I'm spending the night."

My mouth hung open catching flies.

Quen pressed my lower jaw closed. "You did say something about going to bed? Get to it, woman."

I just knew he wasn't expecting sex from a woman who'd been recently discharged from the hospital. But I loved the idea of him bringing me dinner on a tray.

I took the protein drink with me, washed my face, brushed my teeth and climbed into bed. The linens were crisp and clean; Jen's doing. I picked up a magazine from the side of the bed and began flipping through it. There were pictures of Vivica Fox, Halle Berry, Regina King and others on there way up. Women I'd hoped to look like. There was also a photo of Queen Latifah, confident, smiling and beautiful in her bigness. People loved her because she was real. Now there was a woman whose size hadn't hurt her much. It was something to consider.

I was thinking about Queen Latifah when Quen came in balancing a tray in one hand, a dish towel was draped over the other.

"Dinner is now served, madam," he said in a solemn voice.

He whipped off the linen covering the tray and tucked it in my neckline like a bib. On the tray was a vase with a solitary rosebud. I dug into the bowl of soup that smelled delicious and bit into the crusty roll then I uncovered the dish with the main meal. That's how starved I was.

Quen took over spooning soup in my mouth. Every time I opened up to complain the spoon shut me up.

"Good, huh," he said.

I nodded.

The uncovered dish held a scoop of white rice, a chicken breast and broccoli; real food not hospital food. I ate as much as I could but my stomach had shrunk to almost nothing.

"I've got fruit for dessert," Quen offered.

"Can't eat another thing."

"You need to rest, sugar. I'll get rid of this stuff and check on you in a minute."

He collected the tray and took it to the kitchen and was back in minutes to draw the drapes.

"Is it cool enough for you?" he asked, fiddling with the air-conditioning knobs.

"I like it real cool. Where are you sleeping?" I asked drowsily.

"On the sofa."

I was half asleep but not stupid. "Hell, no. You're sleeping right here with me," I said, yawning.

"Not such a good idea, sugar. Too tempting."

I ignored him and pretended to snore.

Quen laughed and climbed into bed beside me. He wrapped his arms around my waist and pulled me closer. My butt was pressed right against his rock-hard stomach.

"Sweet dreams, babe," he said.

When he kissed the nape of my neck and blew softly against my skin, I relaxed. I snuggled against him feeling safe and protected. It was an unusual feeling for me. I didn't do safe easily and protected was an entirely new experience for me.

I must have fallen asleep because when I awoke there was total darkness. I needed to use the bathroom. I slid out from under Quen's arm.

He rolled over muttering something that sounded like, "Joya."

Now I was wide awake and alert. When he said nothing more I was convinced I'd misheard. I looked at my watch. It was going on nine. Quen must be missing work. I needed to wake him up.

I placed a hand on his bare shoulder and shook. His skin felt warm to the touch. He'd shed his shirt during the night and it lay on the wooden floor. I picked it up and shook out the wrinkles.

"Quen you need to get up," I whispered close to his ear.

He snorted and rolled onto his back. I poked his ribs with my index finger.

"Get up. It's late."

One eye squinted open. "What?"

I tapped the face of his watch. "It's going on nine."

He yawned. "So? Come back to bed. I took a couple of days off to be with you."

Another new experience. No one had ever taken time off for me.

"I'll make us coffee," I said, backing out of the room.

"No you won't. Coffee making is my job."

Quen bounded out of bed. He stood before me in his briefs, dark, toned and handsome. My mouth watered just looking at him. He opened the drapes and the bright rays of morning sunshine played across the wooden floors.

"Go clean up and we'll decide where to eat," he said.

Fine by me. I'd loved eating but I'd never been much of a cook.

By the time I'd showered and changed clothes, the meal was already prepared and a delicious aroma filled my nostrils.

"Outside or in?" Quen asked when I stood at the kitchen counter.

"Out."

It promised to be another beautiful Florida day and I didn't want to miss one moment of it. As I wandered outside, I remembered Jen's card and her insistence that I read it. I found the card where I'd left it tucked into the chair cushion and gave it a glance.

"Oh, my God!"

"Problem, sugar?"

"Hell, no. Reason to celebrate. Jen's going to let me write the column by myself one day a week, and she's giving me a raise and credit."

"Congratulations! Now go."

Quen shooed me outside and followed shortly with a tray. He sat it down on a small bistro table and made sure my napkin was in my lap. I sipped on orange juice, ate cereal and nibbled on a boiled egg and unbuttered toast. I was so happy and felt like I would burst.

"Can we walk this off," I suggested, energized and rearing to go.

Quen looked at me sideways. "Sure you're up to it, sugar? Give yourself a day or two to regain your strength and then we'll walk."

"I'm up to it. I've been cooped up inside a smelly hospital for days. I need exercise."

"Okay," he relented. "We'll take it slow, just up the boardwalk a bit, and I'll be holding on to you."

Quen was starting to get on my last nerve. I didn't like being treated like an invalid. On the other hand, it was a good excuse to get up close and personal with him. So I'd milk it for all it was worth.

We managed to get a few feet up the boardwalk before the first person stopped us.

"I heard you were in the hospital," a woman I barely knew said. "It's nice to have a big strong man take care of you." She gave Quen a wink.

I smiled and nodded and held on more tightly to Quen's arm. "Told you people in this town are nosy," I said.

Now who comes sailing by on a bicycle but Joya herself. The basket swinging off her handlebars held fresh produce. She slowed down when she saw us and gave us a shaky smile. I wanted to see how Quen was going to handle this.

"Hi," he said just as if she was a next door neighbor. "How come you're out this early? You never used to be an early bird."

Joya pointed to the basket filled with plump red tomatoes, heads of lettuce and collard greens.

"It's been years since I've been to the Green Market. I wanted to get there early so that I could have my pick. What are you two up to?"

She didn't sound as if it bothered her to see us together.

"Taking a walk," I said. "Let's go as far as the market, Quen?"

"Whatever you want, sugar." He placed an arm around my shoulders and kissed my cheek, steering me away. "See you around, Joya."

Quen had just publicly acknowledged that we were more than friends, but I wanted to hear the magic words, needed to hear them. I needed to know where I stood with him. We'd been dancing around the issue of us for far too long. I'd give it a few minutes then I'd bring it up.

Hand in hand, we wandered through the Green Market. I watched an artist paint the little tents the vendors sold their wares under. Then I bought freshly squeezed juice and shared it with Quen, and we both bought a melon and tangerines. When I stopped to admire a plant, Quen bought the potted hibiscus for me.

"It'll be perfect on the balcony," he said.

Which reminded me it wasn't my balcony and I had stuff in storage I was paying a fortune for. Generous as Jen was, I needed to do something about finding a place to live. Hopefully, the old lady Ida knew was still interested in a rental with option to buy. The last she'd proposed was applying a portion of my rent to offset some of the down payment.

As we started back I decided it was now or never. I took a deep breath.

"Let's sit for a minute." I pointed to a bench on the boardwalk overlooking the ocean.

"How inconsiderate of me not to notice you were getting tired," Quen said.

I wasn't to the point I needed to sit down, but I let him think that. I uncapped the bottle of juice that I was holding, took a sip and offered it to him. Quen took a slug.

Then working up the courage, I said, "Look I'm not sure what's really going on here."

"By that you mean?" I could tell he was uncomfortable.

"I'm not sure what we have. It's like you run hot and cold. Where do you want to go with this?"

There I'd said it. I was done tiptoeing around the issue. When I was lying flat on my back in the hospital I realized that I wasn't getting any younger. I wanted a man and a family, and I didn't want to invest any more time in a friendship that wasn't going to move forward. I was doing this for me, to preserve my heart. I'd already prepared myself to be kicked to the curb.

Quen took a long time answering. The silence made me wish I'd brought the inhaler I hadn't used in weeks.

"Initially I didn't know where I wanted to go with this," he said honestly. "There are so many things I always liked about you. You're fresh, open, honest and make me laugh. Best of all you don't put on airs."

What about finding me attractive? I was attractive. I'd finally found my comfort zone. My personality and sense of humor were two major assets. Somewhere down deep I would always want to be thinner, taller, cuter, but what was really important was I liked me. I now knew I had a lot to give to the right person.

"What I'd like," Quen said, "Is for me and you to really get to know each other, go out a few times, spend time talking, that kind of thing."

"You mean date?" I asked and held my breath.

"Yes, date."

"As in we are free to see other people?"

He looked like I had sucker punched him. I tried to hide my smile.

"Date others if you feel you have to," he said.

He wasn't going to commit. Now I knew what I had to do. Much as I cared about the man I wasn't about to sit around waiting forever. I wanted a relationship and I wanted babies. I wasn't exactly Skinny Minnie but I'd shed enough weight that men previously out of my league might find me attractive. I was doing okay as a Realtor and I had a lot going for me.

Chere Adams was now going to put herself back

on the market. And if Quen Abrahams knew what was good for him he'd get busy. Because I planned on being plenty busy every chance I got.

I was going to work every damn asset I had.

Chapter 20

I decided to give Dickie Dyson another try. When I went in to pay my car payment, I made sure I was wearing an outfit that had Dickie drooling all over himself. It showed enough cleavage to make your eyes pop. And Dickie bit, he asked me out, and I said "yes."

We drove to a nearby town to watch the car races. We sat in the stands watching the Nascar guys, hollering and cheering like fools. Dickie was making a big fool out of himself, jumping up and down and cursing at a driver who didn't seem to have a prayer of even placing. It was all in good fun.

In the two weeks since I'd had the talk with Quen I'd gone out on four dates. None of these men were actually ringing my chimes, but I was getting out and feeling good about myself. And that's what mattered.

I'd managed to work something out with the old lady Ida knew. She was in no hurry to go into an assisted living facility and we planned to talk again after my two months of living rent free at Jen's was up.

Screams now came from the people surrounding me.

"Holy shit!" Dickie said, kicking the seat in front of him and causing the large red-faced man with the beer belly to turn around and glare at him.

"Sorry," Dickie said before the man really got going.

I shot to my feet, joining Dickie, wondering what all the commotion was about. I saw one car up in smoke. It had skidded off the track and was spinning around in circles. The driver was a favorite. The people in the stands, an interesting group, were screaming hysterically and people were running toward the burning car from the pit.

Around me, women of every shape, size and age were dressed in outfits with everything hanging out. The short shorts left little to fantasize about. I'd never seen so much tattooed skin and piercings in my life.

An underdog won the race with two favorites coming in second and third. I knew next to nothing about Nascar racing so most of what was going on had to be explained to me by Dickie.

Afterward we took the long way back to Flamingo Beach. Dickie drove one of his Mercedes with the sunroof open and we tooled down A1A where all the rich people lived.

"Imagine having that kind of money," I said, gazing out at the big houses that sat on the water, and wishing I were with Quen.

"I'm getting there, babe."

I knew that was to tempt me. Dickie still couldn't get over the fact that I didn't want to sleep with him and that I wasn't overly impressed with the greenbacks he threw around. Quen had spoiled me for the Dickies of the world.

We were still working out together and Quen called occasionally, supposedly to chat. But there had been no movement forward which led me to believe he was still confused. My patience was wearing thin.

I had a rapidly ticking biological clock and didn't want to wait around until some man got to me. I loved Quen but I wasn't about to be any man's lady in waiting. Especially when I didn't know what I was waiting for.

Dickie pulled over to the side of the road and parked behind a line of cars.

I raised my eyebrows. "What are we doing?"

"Taking a walk along the beach." He ran his fingers through what used to be called a Jheri curl back in the day. Now it was some other kind of processing. I just hoped he wasn't planning on getting romantic.

We walked down a steep flight of steps and toward the beach. Several other people had the same idea because the sands were fairly crowded. There were teenagers flying kites and toddlers holding on to parents and wading in the water. They looked so cute. I wanted one of those rug rats.

I looked enviously at the handful of couples sitting on the sand and those walking hand in hand. It was a mistake coming here with Richard when I only wanted to be with Quen. The setting and the couples reminded me of what I didn't have—a relationship with someone who loved me.

"Richard, I'm not feeling well," I lied. "Would you mind taking me home?"

Richard looked over at me and frowned. "Must be

sunstroke from all that time out in the sun." At times he could be dense.

Let him call it whatever he wanted so his ego wouldn't get crushed. We made a U-turn and headed up the steps.

Give Dickie Dyson credit, he was a good sport. He headed west and picked up I95 in order to get me home fast. As luck would have it, no sooner had we pulled up in front of my building, guess who was coming out? Quen.

"Feel better," Dickie shouted from the convertible Mercedes as I crossed the lot and headed for the lobby.

"Thanks. I had a nice time," I shouted back. "See you soon."

Richard took off burning rubber.

At the front door Quen stopped me. "I came by to see you," he said, placing a hand on my arm. Where he touched me tingled.

"Any particular reason why?"

"Can I come up and talk?"

"Sure."

I was playing it cool but my stomach was fluttering like a butterfly coming out of its cocoon.

"You look nice," Quen said.

I thanked him. I knew I looked good. I'd just

gotten my hair straightened and I'd brushed it back off my face and put in those little pins that sparkled. I had cute black walking shorts on with cuffs that came in a size sixteen, and made me look trim. And I had a hot pink T-shirt on that came down to my thighs. Pink looked good against my dark skin.

We rode the elevator in silence to the fifth floor.

Inside the apartment, Quen said, "Tell me you're not seeing Richard Dyson."

I stared him down. "What's it to you?"

Quen crossed to the sliders and looked down on the boardwalk. "It's just that I don't want Richard playing you. The man gets around."

I sank onto the couch, kicked off my black sandals and put both feet on the ottoman. "I'm a big girl. I can handle Dickie."

"I don't like it that you're seeing him."

I cut my eyes at him. "What's it to you?"

"I'm just not happy about you spending time in that man's company."

"And just why is that?"

Quen turned around, and I swear I'd never seen so much pain in a man's eyes. It almost made me feel guilty. "Let me break it down for you," he said. "I didn't realize how much I cared about you until we stopped hanging out."

That got me off the couch and walking toward him. I practically got in his face. "What are you going to do about it?"

He squared his shoulders. "I've already given it a lot of thought. I think we should start dating exclusively."

My heart jumped but I didn't want to appear too anxious. Besides he still hadn't told me he loved me.

"Hmm. I've been thinking, too," I said, "And thinking maybe we shouldn't waste each others time if you're not serious. I'm of the age where I am looking for marriage and babies."

Quen gulped a bit but to his credit pulled himself together, "Got to start somewhere, sugar. And the first step is dating."

That was enough for me. When he reached an arm to pull me close I didn't stop him. And when he dipped his head and those full lips captured my mouth I just about melted. Our tongues touched, mingled and our hands explored, groping each other's skin. Quen cupped my buttocks and pulled me closer. I felt how much I excited him.

He still hadn't said what I wanted to hear. So I pulled away from him when he was breathing really hard.

"You're forgetting to tell me something," I said.

He gulped again. "Good lord woman you drive a hard bargain. Haven't I shown you enough?"

"Not good enough." I wanted more. Needed more.

We stared at each other.

"Is it I love you, you need to hear?" he asked.

"Exactly right, and mean it, too."

Quen gave me a great big squeeze. "Sugar, I have loved you from the moment I realized that you weren't my sister. You had discipline and drive and were bent and determined to get your weight in check, regardless of what that took. You put a lot of energy into improving your life and you took the necessary steps to do so. I don't just love you, baby, I respect and admire you."

My eyes watered and I let the tears flow. Quen had said much more than I'd expected of him. I'd never had a man respect me, nor accept me for the person I am. Heck, it had taken me awhile and a few hard knocks to accept the real me, and I was the person who thought she knew who she was. Big, bad, bold, beautiful, Chere.

It had taken Quen's loving to help me find the inner strengths that I didn't know I had, and to realize beauty was far more than your outer appearance. It came from deep within.

While Quen might not know it yet, I planned on

marrying the fool. I couldn't think of anyone who would make a better husband and father.

"I love you, Quen Abrahams," I said between tears.

"And I love you."

He handed me his handkerchief and I wiped my eyes. Then he took me by the hand and we headed for my room.

Life just didn't get much sweeter than this.